ADVANCE PRAISE FOR
THE SALINGER CONTRACT

"Skewers pretensions of writers and writing, editors and publishers—and perhaps audiences—in a literary thriller. . . . Marvelously intriguing." —*Kirkus Reviews*, starred review

"Whom do we really write for and why? Langer's mad-genius look at creativity, publishing, and the difference between what we do for love and what we're forced to do for money, plumbs the dark side of inspiration with funhouse aplomb. Dizzyingly brilliant, with prose as clear as a rushing stream." —Caroline Leavitt, *New York Times* bestselling author of *Pictures of You and Is This Tomorrow*

"'Revelatory. Keeps all its secrets to the end, which is a whopper.' . . . Wait. That's a blurb for a novel within Adam Langer's novel. But it applies just as well to *The Salinger Contract*, Langer's latest nervy excursion on the boundary between fiction, non-fiction, and literary gamesmanship. A lot of fun, up to and including that whopper . . ." —Ben Yagoda, author of *How to Not Write Bad: The Most Common Writing Problems and the Best Ways to Avoid Them* and *Memoir: A History*

"In *The Salinger Contract*, Adam Langer serves as chief anthropologist, guiding us deftly through the tribal customs of the literary world—its longings, follies, disappointments, and secret obsessions. Like nesting boxes, this novel is neat with puzzles and intrigue. I couldn't put it down—a cliché I can't resist!" —Patricia Henley, National Book Award–nominated author of *Other Heartbreaks* and *In the River Sweet*

"*The Salinger Contract* is at once a mercilessly readable thriller, and a sly commentary on the state of the artist in the modern world. Langer undermines the reader's expectation at every twist and turn, proving, as only the best thrillers do, that nothing is what it seems." —Jonathan Evison, author of *West of Here* and *The Revised Fundamentals of Caregiving*

PRAISE FOR THE WRITING
OF ADAM LANGER

The Thieves of Manhattan

"*The Thieves of Manhattan* is a sly and cutting riff on the book-publishing world that is quite funny unless you happen to be an author, in which case the novel will make you consider a more sensible profession—like being a rodeo clown, for example, or a crab-fisherman in the Bering Sea." —Carl Hiaasen

"Takes us to places that fiction dares not tread. Bold brave worrying work from a wonderful wunderkind!" —Laura Albert, otherwise known as JT LeRoy, author of *Sarah* and *The Heart Is Deceitful Beyond All Things*

"I loved this book—it's both laugh-out-loud funny and satisfyingly snarky about the state of publishing these days. Both writers and readers should find this cautionary tale a delight to read." —Nancy Pearl, author of *Book Lust*

"A page-turning thriller, a lacerating lampoon of the literary life, and a powerful tribute to the art and craft of fakery." —Clifford Irving, author of *The Autobiography of Howard Hughes* and *The Hoax*

"Wonderfully mischievous . . . as soulful and morally committed as it is funny and clever." —*Los Angeles Times*

"*The Thieves of Manhattan* is near perfection . . . an exciting read that will put a dark smile on the face of anyone discouraged by the downward spiral of literature." —The Daily Beast

"*The Thieves of Manhattan* is a marvelous yarn, a glorious paean to good books and to those who shepherd them into the world, a tale of redemption as cheering as Michael Chabon's *Wonder Boys*." —*Chicago Tribune*

"*The Thieves of Manhattan* may be to publishing what Joseph Heller's *Catch-22* was to the military." —Associated Press

"Love and art merge with cheerful cynicism in Langer's madcap skewering of New York's personality-mad publishing industry." —*Vogue*

"Part *Bright Lights, Big City*, part *The Grifters*, this delicious satire of the literary world is peppered with slang so trendy a glossary is included." —*Publishers Weekly*, starred review

Ellington Boulevard

"Langer has that rare combination of fierce intelligence, wicked wit and the ability to make you turn pages at wrist-splintering speed. This is one of the very best recent novels of New York." —*USA Today*

"Wacky and wonderful . . . a quintessentially New York tale." —*Daily News* (New York)

"A New York City novel par excellence." —*Kirkus Reviews*, starred review

"Adam Langer lifts the lid off the top of New York City and lets us see, close up, and terribly personally, the cosmopolitan complexity of the city that never sleeps alone . . . The composition and orchestration that Mr. Langer has gifted us with would have delighted the Duke himself." —Larry Gelbart, creator of *M*A*S*H*, co-screenwriter of *Tootsie*, and Tony Award–winning author of *City of Angels* and *A Funny Thing Happened on the Way to the Forum*

"Adam Langer's new novel, *Ellington Boulevard*, captures all of Manhattan's quirky insanity with great style and a huge amount of fun." —Barbara Corcoran

"Adam Langer took me on a wonderful trip all over the Upper West Side of Manhattan. The reader will meet musicians, actors, and even a dog named Herbie Mann—open the cover, read, and enjoy! This is his best book yet." —Eli Wallach, actor

"Adam Langer, who is either a genius or a schizophrenic, inhabits his characters—from a pregnant woman to a pigeon—with brilliant stealth and lovable insouciance. Finally a book has come along that has gotten me excited about reading and even New York again." —Jennifer Belle, author of *High Maintenance* and *Little Stalker*

"I laughed out loud throughout this simultaneously cynical and sentimental New York fairy tale with a love for off-Broadway musicals and the seventeen-key clarinet, and a profound understanding of the importance of dogs." —Stephen Schwartz, Academy Award–winning lyricist and composer for *Wicked*, *Godspell*, *Pippin*, and *The Prince of Egypt*

Crossing California

"A work of unusual mastery, compassion, insight, and wit." —Gary Shteyngart

"In his ambitious, irresistible debut, Langer packs in more hilarious and agonizing moments than most writers manage in a lifetime." —*Entertainment Weekly*

"A teeming, hilarious, ambitious, and almost blindingly vivid portrait of a very particular Chicago at a very particular time." —*Newsday*

"*Crossing California* is the most vivid novel about Chicago since Saul Bellow's *Herzog* and the most ambitious debut set in Chicago since Philip Roth's *Letting Go*." —*Chicago Tribune*

"In this rich saga worthy of Philip Roth and Anthony Trollope, Langer has finally given us [Chicago's] definitive document." —*Los Angeles Times*

"Langer drills to the core of people—five gifted teens and their clueless elders in 1979–81 Chicago—as deeply as Jonathan Franzen did in *The Corrections*." —*People*

"A brilliant debut." —*Publishers Weekly*

The
SALINGER
CONTRACT

The
SALINGER
CONTRACT

a novel

Adam Langer

OPEN ROAD
INTEGRATED MEDIA
NEW YORK

Cover design by Mauricio Díaz

978-1-4532-9794-0

Published in 2013 by Open Road Integrated Media, Inc.
345 Hudson Street
New York, NY 10014
www.openroadmedia.com

For Wendy Salinger, my favorite writer with that surname

As always, for Beate, Nora, and Solveig

As for my parents, I hope someday they'll forgive me for the secrets I have revealed here

The
SALINGER
CONTRACT

Promise me that if ever I find the courage to think like a hero,
you will act like a merely decent human being.

John Le Carré, *The Russia House*

I:
Upon Signing

Forgive me, Father, for I know exactly what I did.
Forgive me, Father, for I know all that I still must do.

Conner Joyce, *Ice Locker*

1

I never believed a book could save your life. It makes sense that Conner Joyce would be the one who changed my mind about that. The story of how one book saved me while another nearly killed Conner began, appropriately enough, in a bookstore—to be more precise, at Borders in Bloomington, Indiana, where I saw a poster with Conner's picture on it. By then, I had nearly forgotten Conner. I had figured I was done with books.

After my magazine, *Lit,* folded half a dozen years earlier and I lost my plum position as books editor, I pretty much stopped reading contemporary fiction, particularly crime novels like the ones Conner wrote. I may have spent a fair amount of time decrying the demise of America's reading culture, but it wasn't like I was helping to improve the situation. My wife had a good gig at the university, and we had two young daughters: Ramona, age six, who was just starting chapter books, and Beatrice, two and a half, who was a voracious consumer of picture books, and that's pretty much all I found time to read. As far as I was concerned, the interesting part of my life was over.

When I lived in New York and worked for the magazine, I wrote author profiles—pieces of 1,500 to 2,000 words that allowed authors to tell their stories in their own words in an environment in which they felt comfortable. I walked the Freedom Trail in Boston with Dennis Lehane; rode the Wonder Wheel at Coney Island with E. L. Doctorow; attended a Springsteen concert with Margaret Atwood; and went camping in the Pocono Mountains with Conner Joyce and his wife, Angela De La Roja. Not exactly hard-hitting journalism, but the authors usually liked the articles because I printed their quotes verbatim and cleaned up their swearwords if they asked. Plus, the pictures that accompanied the articles were extremely flattering. Hardly anyone had ever called Maurice Sendak or Stephen King handsome before they saw my profiles. And even Conner Joyce—once named one of America's Sexiest Writers by *People* magazine—told me he'd never seen a better photo of himself.

My *Lit* profiles usually conformed to one of two basic templates—either an author was exactly like the characters he wrote about in his books or (surprise!) he was nothing like them. My profile of Conner ("His Aim Is True: How Stories Saved Conner Joyce's Life") fell somewhere between the two: though I sensed he was too compassionate and earnest to commit the crimes he wrote, the humanity of his characters was clearly his own.

When I interviewed Conner in Pennsylvania, we talked a lot about books. I turned him on to my favorite authors, Italo Calvino, Alain Robbe-Grillet, and José Saramago; he tried to convince me of the merits of Jarosław Dudek and J. D. Salinger. Most of his favorite authors were recluses, he said. He admired writers whose own stories were as interesting as the ones they wrote. He loved the mystery of Salinger, holed up in his home in Cornish, New Hampshire, refusing to publish for more than forty years. He was captivated by the life of Jarosław Dudek, the Olympic shot-put silver medalist and Ministry of Internal Affairs functionary who won just about every international literary award with his only novel, *Other Countries, Other Lives*, then disappeared shortly after the fall of the Berlin Wall. Conner had read every biography ever written about B. Traven, the author of *The Treasure of the Sierra Madre*, who concealed his identity using anagrammatic pseudonyms such as Ret Marut and Hal Croves and was rumored to be the son of Kaiser Wilhelm. He had spent hours admiring and puzzling over the last-known photographs of Thomas Pynchon taken at Cornell University. He had written a high school research paper about Roland Cephus, the unofficial poet laureate of the Black Panther movement who had gone underground after the 1971 publication of *A Molotov Manifesto*.

As a boy and as a teenager, Conner had written letters to the agents and publishers for Dudek, Salinger, Pynchon, and Harper Lee. He hoped his heartfelt appreciation of *To Kill a Mockingbird* and Atticus Finch would make Lee break her silence and tell him about her quiet little existence in Monroeville, Alabama. He never received responses, yet he fantasized about meeting those writers, and he still wondered what it would be like to be so intriguing that people would actually care if he disappeared.

The way I remembered him, Conner was one of the good guys—a big, earnest Irish-Catholic from a family of police sergeants, fire department captains, Eagle Scouts, and Navy vets. The kind of guy you wanted to captain your ball team, to help talk your way out of a bad neighborhood after dark, or to pilot your plane through rough weather. He was one of the few authors I interviewed who actually seemed more interested in hearing about me than I was in hearing about him.

In the time we spent together, even though I told him I didn't really like talking about it, somehow he got me to tell him my whole family story—what I knew of it anyway: being born to a single mom; growing up in a two-bedroom apartment on West Farragut Street on Chicago's drab north side; putting myself through college at UIC; refusing my mother's offers of money because I knew how cash-strapped she was; working as a waiter, a writer for CBS Radio, and a freelancer for various alternative newspapers such as *Neon*, *Strong Coffee*, and *The Reader*; meeting my future wife, Sabine, one night at the Lakeview café called Java Jive when she was on a study-abroad program and I was working behind the counter, long before anyone had heard the word "barista"; moving with Sabine to New York, where she went to grad school and I edited *Lit*. I told Conner about my vain attempts to track down my birth father, about my tight-lipped mother, Trudy Herstein, a longtime worker for the Tribune Company who cocooned herself in silence whenever I asked about her life before I was born. When I told Conner I was writing a novel about my search for my father, he said it sounded like a great book and he'd love to read it.

When I finished writing up the interview, I let him approve his quotes before I published the piece. He didn't ask me to change anything, and only requested that I airbrush the cigarette from his pictures. He wanted to be a dad someday, he said, and didn't want his kid to see him smoking. I got into a big fight about it with my publisher, M. J. Thacker, who had been trying to get Philip Morris to take out a full-page ad, but ultimately, I won that battle for Conner.

When I needed someone to endorse *Nine Fathers*—my first and, to date, only novel—I sent out about a dozen e-mails and letters to various authors I had interviewed. And though, at the time, Conner was one of the biggest names among them, he was first to respond. He didn't act busy and self-important like E. L. Doctorow, whose agent told me he didn't have the time to devote to a first-time author. And he wasn't one of those patronizing assholes like Blade Markham, who tossed off something in half a minute, misspelling my name and getting the title wrong (*Nineteen Fathers*) just to let me know he was doing me a favor and hadn't read a word. From what Conner wrote, you could tell he had actually read the whole book, had thought about it carefully, and apparently understood more about me from reading it than I did from writing it. "Revelatory," he wrote. "Keeps all its secrets until the very end, which is a whopper." I thought the blurb was a little over the top, but it looked good on the jacket.

The last time I had seen Conner—at the New York premiere for the movie adaptation of his debut novel, *Devil Shotgun: A Cole Padgett Thriller*—he told me to give him a ring whenever I passed through Pennsylvania, and he didn't seem like the type of guy who would bullshit about something like that. But then my wife got her faculty gig here at the Graduate School of Foreign Policy and we moved away. I fell out of touch with most of my old contacts, and I barely spent any time in Manhattan, let alone in Philadelphia. When *Nine Fathers* was published, I kept wishing vainly that my old assistant, Miriam, who now worked as one of Terry Gross's producers for *Fresh Air*, would book me for an interview in Philly so that I would have an excuse to call Conner up.

But that never happened. Conner had his life writing crime novels in Pennsylvania; I sat on my front porch with my laptop, or in my wife's library carrel in Indiana, surfing other people's iTunes playlists and trying to think of ideas for a follow-up to *Nine Fathers* that wouldn't offend my mother.

When I saw the poster at Borders advertising Conner's reading, I was with Beatrice. We were shopping to replace her copy of *Knuffle Bunny Too*, which I had accidentally washed along with a load of her cloth diapers. This had become my life—cooking dinner, walking the dog, squiring Ramona to school and Beatrice to day care, and taking the two of them to cafés, ballet class, gymnastics, play dates, birthday parties, and bookstores. I would write a few pages per day on drafts of stories and books I wasn't sure I would ever finish while my spouse slaved away on the syllabi, scholarly articles, and book proposals that would win her tenure so that we would never have to worry about health insurance or the price of college tuition.

Dr. Sabine Krummel, my spouse, was a graduate of both the Freie Universität of Berlin and Columbia University. She had published one book with Routledge Press (*Fusion and Diffusion: A Network Analysis of How Rules Governing Nuclear Power Safety Procedures Transfer Across European Member State Borders*) and had a contract for her follow-up book with Cambridge University Press (*Auto-stimulation and Autonomy Under Import Substitution in Postcolonial Society*). She was "a shoo-in for tenure, man," at least according to her dreadlocked, eternally stoned department chair, Dr. Joel Getty, who was better known by his nickname, "Spag."

Occasionally, I groused to Sabine about our life in Bloomington, and how much it paled in comparison to the life we had led in Manhattan. To keep ourselves amused, we kept a private blog under the pen name Buck Floomington. We wrote awful, nasty stuff about Sabine's colleagues that we never shared with anyone: who was sleeping with whom, who liked to go shooting at the target range behind Brad's Guns outside Indianapolis, who had threatened his family with a chainsaw, who hired only Asian women to serve as his work studies, who kept a shrine to basketball coach Bobby Knight in his rec room, who had gotten banned from the strip mall massage studio for demanding a hand job . . . It was cathartic. Sometimes, in the desolate, insular heartland, you do whatever you can to keep your mind alive.

Still, what from the outside may have looked like complacency actually felt a lot like security. Bloomington was a quiet college town that may have offered little, but it also expected little in return. And though most of the faculty spouses I knew had either settled or given up, there was a certain comfort in surrender. Sure, I could have finished a second book or freelanced this or that article. I could have competed for a lecturing gig at Butler University or Ivy Tech or for an editorial job at some magazine, such as *Indianapolis Monthly* or *Bloom*. But if I wanted to spend my days literally bleaching the shit out of diapers and mastering the art of vegetarian cooking with the aid of cookbooks by the only authors I read anymore, Mark Bittman and Deborah Madison, then that was fine too.

The Bloomington Borders, located next to a FedEx Kinko's and across from a Panera Bread in the College Mall, was going out of business, and all kids' books were 50 percent off. Beatrice and I were stocking up on Mo Willems and Dr. Seuss books when I saw the color Xerox of Conner, smack dab in the center aisle. The shot looked just like the ones we had used in *Lit*—Conner with a full head of black curls and five o'clock shadow, his serious, pale-blue eyes staring straight at you as if he had something important to say and was hoping you'd give him the time to listen. He was wearing a sport coat, a pressed light-blue shirt, and boots. His hands were stuffed in the pockets of his jeans, one thumb tucked in a belt loop. On one of his wrists was an expensive-looking watch. He looked tough and earnest, the publishing world's answer to Josh Brolin— what John Irving should have looked like but didn't. I was studying Conner's photo when I noticed Beatrice tugging on my sleeve.

"Who's that person you keep staring at?" she asked.

"Guy I used to know," I said. "His name is Conner."

"Is he your friend?"

I said I wasn't sure, but I would probably go to his reading, and maybe I would ask him to come by our house for dinner or dessert. "Maybe you'll get to meet him too," I said. "Wouldn't you like that?"

"No." Beatrice began to toddle off in the direction of the children's section. She seemed a bit scared of the guy in the picture, or perhaps scared of what she thought my friendship with him might bring. But I couldn't begin to imagine what could possibly frighten her about a good-looking, all-American guy like Conner, or about the fact that I still wanted to be his friend.

2

As it turned out, Conner didn't come to our house for dinner or dessert; it was a school night and the kids needed to be in bed by nine. But I did go to the reading. I had figured I would sit in the back and mill about until he was done greeting his fans. But the turnout was poor. Really poor. Authors tend to exaggerate the number of people who come to readings, or at least I do. Usually, if you divide by three, you get the true figure. When you say only seven or eight people showed up, everyone gets depressed, uncomfortable, and judgmental, particularly in a college town where no one regards writing books as an actual career.

"Right, but what do you do for money?" my wife's colleagues continually asked me when I trailed along to departmental parties or when I ran into them at Lowes or Home Depot or Best Buy. In their line of work, or whatever they did that passed for work, writing was just one of the many things you did to keep your job—you didn't expect anybody to read what you wrote, let alone pay you for it. After all, you'd gotten your job by convincing your employers you'd read hundreds of books they probably hadn't read themselves. When you told these folks honestly that you had a lousy turnout, they tended to guess twenty-five or thirty people came. But when I showed up at the Bloomington Borders for the Conner Joyce reading, only eight people were there, including the events coordinator.

On the metal folding chairs positioned in rows in front of a podium and a signing table were a pair of trampy white women in their late thirties or early forties; they were wearing tight, sequined blue jeans and were holding copies of *People* magazine's bachelors issue, circa 2005, for Conner to sign. There was the de rigueur weedy, sunlight-averse guy with copies of each of Conner's books stacked in a wheeled pushcart, undoubtedly hoping to move autographed first editions on eBay ("Just your signature. No inscription," he said). There was a doughy lady in her early fifties with a library copy of *Ice Locker* and a digital camera so she could take a photo of Conner for her blog, *Authors Are My Weakness*. Conner gamely agreed, but after she snapped the pic and he mentioned his wife, she didn't stick around.

A homeless dude was sprawled across three chairs in the front row; there was a white boy with baggy jeans, a turned-around vintage Montreal Expos baseball cap, dragon tattoos on his shoulders, and an iPod, reading a copy of *XXL*; an Asian girl with a mug of coffee was studying for the SATs and leaving coffee rings on her test-prep book. None of them seemed to know who Conner was. Maybe some had seen the straight-to-DVD movie of *Devil Shotgun* (pretty good performance by Mark Ruffalo in the lead role of Detective Cole Padgett if you feel like streaming it on Netflix), but they didn't seem aware the author was in the store. The other customers in Borders were either purchasing coffee, reading books and magazines they hadn't paid for and weren't intending to pay for, or buying discounted books by James Patterson, Stephenie Meyer, or Margot Hetley.

Conner, wearing his traditional getup of a good heavy sport coat, jeans, and a light-blue button-down shirt, was adjusting the microphone at his podium and studying a sheet of prepared remarks through a set of half glasses. Those glasses were the only sign he had aged at all since I had last seen him. Otherwise, he looked eager and energetic, smiling all dimples at the women in the front row seated next to the homeless guy. Conner smiled as if he didn't notice how small the crowd was, or as if he felt flattered that anyone would go out of his or her way to hear him speak. The humility I have always worked so hard to affect seemed to come naturally to Conner.

I didn't know whether I would be doing Conner more of a service by sitting up front and making the crowd look bigger or by sneaking out and pretending I hadn't noticed how few people were there. But before I had decided, Conner caught sight of me by the bestsellers shelf, where I was flipping through *The Fearsome Shallow*—the eighth book in Margot Hetley's Wizard Vampire Chronicles series. I was wondering how Ms. Hetley, who seemed to occupy just about every slot on the *New York Times* hardback, paperback, and e-book bestseller lists, had managed to wring eight five-hundred-page installments out of the concept of wars between rival gangs of vampires and wizards when it seemed obvious to me that all a wizard would have to do to kick a vampire's ass was pounce on it during the day while it was sleeping. How could anyone take this stuff seriously, I wondered. Hetley's graphic depictions of wizard-on-vampire sex, which was creating a bloodthirsty, mutant race of evil, soulless "vampards," seemed absurd. I was still scanning Hetley's book when Conner's voice boomed out, as loud as if he had been speaking over the public address system.

"I was wondering if you'd come out of hiding, buddy; I was thinking maybe I was gonna hafta track you down," he said with a laugh. I put down the Hetley book as Conner bounded over and pulled me into a hug. He smelled like dry-cleaned sport coat and he-man cologne, the musky sort that an old-time ballplayer might have worn for a night on the town. He kissed my cheek and I could feel his stubble. "What're you doin' afterwards, bud?" he asked. "You got some time to hang out?"

I told him I didn't have plans, but since I hadn't called to tell him I would be there, I would understand if he were too busy to have more than one drink.

"Do I look too busy?" he asked. "I've been in this town all day and just about all I've seen is the inside of my hotel room, the quad, and the frickin' food court. It ain't like the old days, my friend; writing books is a tough way to make a buck."

"When were the old days?" I asked.

"'Bout six years ago," he said. "Maybe a little more."

I nodded. "Yeah. That's probably about when my magazine folded and Sabine and I moved here. But haven't you at least done a couple of interviews? Maybe a photo shoot?"

"Not even one, dude."

"Well, it's a sleepy little college town," I said. "Only reason anyone moves here is because of the university or because they like basketball or the movie *Breaking Away*."

Conner smiled. "Yeah, I liked that movie too," he said, then shook his head. "No, the whole book tour's been like this." He said he had traveled to ten cities and the only one left on his itinerary was my hometown—Chicago. Everywhere he had gone, the situation had been pretty much the same. Half a dozen people had attended in Cincinnati, ten each in Milwaukee and Louisville. In Madison, only one guy had come to hear him read at a shopping mall Barnes

& Noble and Conner wound up taking that guy, his driver, and his media escort out to dinner. So far, the biggest crowd had been in Manhattan, where thirty people had shown up at the Union Square Barnes & Noble, but Conner's editor Shajilah "Shascha" Schapiro had brought half her office with her and she had been expecting to see a whole lot more people she *didn't* know.

"Frankly," Conner said, "I was kinda hoping to make a better impression on Shascha. We're buds and all, but that doesn't mean she'll keep laying out cash to publish my books." He said he didn't understand why Shascha and her publicity and marketing department were spending all this dough on his hotels, meals, and business-class plane tickets when it looked as if they weren't spending any on promoting the actual book. As far as he was concerned, he'd rather sleep in a YMCA, ride Greyhound, and eat at Mickey D's if they would advertise. He didn't want to seem ungrateful, but he had better things to do than sign half a dozen books in a chain bookstore in a middle-American burg; he had left Angie at home with their son, Atticus, and if he wasn't doing anything useful, he'd rather be home. He hated the idea of becoming the sort of father who was too busy to spend time with his son.

"Kinda like your dad," he said. "Sorry, man. I know you don't like talking about that shit. No offense."

"None taken; you're right," I said, remembering I had told him all about my lonesome boyhood. "Anyway," I added, "you've got a son now. Congratulations."

"Yeah, a son." He looked at me with what seemed to be genuine regret. "Man," he said, "it has been a while, hasn't it? How long?"

"About seven years, something like that," I said. "I've got two kids now."

"Shit, two? Why didn't you tell me?"

"I just figured you'd be busy." I wondered why he seemed to think we were better friends than I imagined we were.

"Yeah." Conner looked around at the sparse crowd with a smirk. "Real busy."

The events coordinator approached us. She was a dowdy woman of an indeterminate age. Her badge said Cathy-Anne, and she looked as though she would have preferred to be managing a Best Buy or a Target, which was most probably what she would wind up doing when this store went out of business at the end of the month.

"Do you want to do the reading now, Mr. Joyce? Or do you want to wait a few more minutes to see if anybody else comes?" she asked.

Conner sighed. "What do you wanna do?" he asked.

"Let's go," she said.

Conner told me to make sure I stuck around afterward, then slapped me on the shoulder as if he had just bested me in a game of hoops. He approached the podium, put his half glasses back on, cracked open a copy of his book, and leaned into the microphone. I took my seat in an empty row near the back, and listened to the first lines of *Ice Locker*:

"Cole Padgett stepped into the darkened confessional booth. 'Forgive me, Father, for I know exactly what I've done. Forgive me, Father, for all that I still must do.'"

3

I wish I could tell you that a whole lot more people showed up after Conner started reading, but only one other person did. I wish I could report that Conner sold or signed more than four books aside from the one I bought. I wish I could say that Cathy-Anne didn't box up the rest of the books to send back to Conner's publisher. I wish Cathy-Anne had been thoughtful enough to turn off or at least turn down "Tubular Bells," which was tinkle-tinking ominously throughout the store, and I wish half of Conner's sentences weren't drowned out by espresso and Frappuccino machines.

I wish, too, that everyone who didn't come to Conner's reading were missing something special, that Conner's reading of *Ice Locker*, the latest in his Cole Padgett series, was a mind-blowing experience. But Conner had never been much of a reader. He had a rich basso-profundo but used it uncertainly, like a timid father called upon to speak at his son's confirmation, trying to get through the damn thing without embarrassing his family. At one point in his career, someone had apparently coached Conner in how to read in front of an audience. But whenever he made a supposedly dramatic gesture—say, twirling his right hand to represent smoke rising from the barrel of a .45 caliber gun, or holstering that weapon, which he made out of a thumb and two fingers—it seemed phony and labored, as if practiced in front of a mirror. His vocal cadence shifted between embarrassingly emotive and painfully monotonous. The real trouble, however, wasn't how Conner was reading, but what he was reading. Sure, the writing itself was lucid, crisp, and terse as always, but there was something rote about it, as if he had written this sort of material many times before, which, of course, he had.

This Cole Padgett novel was another of Conner's honest-cop-stuck-in-a-corrupt-system tales. He had written a serial-killer novel in this vein, and an espionage plot; this one happened to be a heist story like his first, *Devil Shotgun*. But the characters, themes, struggles, and Catholic guilt were the same as always. Conner's criminals were rarely habitual offenders; they were basically honest people pushed to their limits, forced to make choices they wouldn't have made under ordinary circumstances. The villain in *Ice Locker* was Cole Padgett's immediate superior, who had been a heroic figure in a few of Conner's previous thrillers. The titular location was where he had been storing evidence of the unsolved crimes he had actually been committing. As was always the case, the villain wasn't some evil outside force; the enemy was within.

Familiar stuff, to be sure, even when Conner had begun his career. But what had initially differentiated Conner's work within his genre was his copious attention to detail. He had become known for his dogged, painstakingly accurate research and his ruthlessly honest portrayal of the gray areas in the traditionally black-and-white world of cops versus robbers. He was well-versed in this topic, knew about it through his work as a beat reporter for the *New York Daily News* and through fictionalizing the stories his wife, Angie, had told him about life as a crime-scene investigator for the NYPD.

"I always wanted to get every detail right," he had told me when I interviewed him. "When I worked for the *Daily News*, I talked to people who had never been in the newspaper before and might never be in the newspaper again. And, man, I wanted to make sure the one time I quoted them, I got everything they said right. I wanted every last spelling, every last detail, to be on target."

But the world had changed since Conner had started writing. Now everyone who had watched *CSI* had become an expert in forensics, and people expected this sort of detailed approach from all authors, not just him. Careful readers began finding minor errors in Conner's work—plot discrepancies, misspelled street names, outdated cop slang—and posted them on fan sites and in online reviews, which were usually less forgiving than print reviews were. Plus, the knowledge on which Conner had based his first books was stale. He hadn't worked at the *Daily News* in nearly a decade, and Angie had quit working for the NYPD after she and Conner had gotten married. *Devil Shotgun* had been a post-9/11 book, the story of a man who committed thefts while adopting the identities of people who had disappeared during the collapse of the Twin Towers. The book had captured a certain moment in American history; but Osama bin Laden was dead, the Bush era was over, and the anxieties of that particular time seemed to belong to the past every bit as much as Conner Joyce's fiction.

These days, Americans were facing different anxieties. The economy was in the tank—the Clearance and Everything Must Go! signs in Borders attested to that fact. The culture had grown increasingly cynical and self-referential, and whether or not Conner Joyce's conflicted hero might have to rob a bank in order to save a hostage's life and find evidence that would prove the case against his boss seemed like a petty concern. These days, you did what you had to do to feed yourself and protect your family.

Conner performed better in the sadly brief Q&A period. Here, his humility, honesty, and enthusiasm came to the fore as he effused about nearly every author who had influenced him. Salinger? "So goddamn honest, man. Like he's talking right *to* you." Tolstoy? "He makes you think it's all happening *right now*, even though he wrote more than a *hundred years ago, man*." Dudek? "How could any-one who survived such dark times find so much humor in them?" Cephus? "It's a crime that his works are out of print now." Conner even gave me a shout-out—"That's a real talent you got living here, a real big name; check him out. C'mon, let's hear it." He asked me to stand up (I did) and take a bow (I didn't). As for his own writing, though, he didn't want to talk about it—not at Borders, and not when I was hanging out with him afterward.

Conner had a driver for the evening—a chauffeur in a shabby black uniform driving an even shabbier black stretch limo, another needless expense. But when I told Conner I would happily drive him back to his hotel when we were done for the night, he slipped the chauffeur a twenty and told him to head home and pick him up at the Indiana Memorial Union at six a.m. so he could catch his flight for Chicago, the last stop on his tour.

"Shit, I know I've lost something," he told me. "There's a reason my books aren't selling anymore. And yeah, I could rationalize the whole thing and say it's because people don't read as much as they used to, or because they're too distracted by their iPods, iPhones, and iPads, or whatever the hell people have now, or because the economy's gone to hell and people don't have money to spend on books, or because people who still like to read just want to read about wizards, vampires, and shit like that. But that's not the whole story. I gotta be honest with you, man, and with myself, too. There's a hell of a lot more to it than that."

We were sitting at an outdoor table at the Upland Brewing Company. Most of the tables were empty even though it was a lovely night. The inside tables were jammed. *Monday Night Football* fans were watching the Colts take on New England. This was one of the things I griped about consistently on the Buck Floomington blog. People don't go outside in this town. Porches were littered with unused lawn furniture. After dinner, my kids were the only ones on the playground. Some of my wife's colleagues even bought houses on large properties surrounded by tall trees to keep passersby from knowing there were children inside.

Conner and I were splitting a plate of pita and hummus. He was drinking a dark beer while I drank club soda—since Ramona was born, I had probably consumed three beers total. The idea of alcohol had nearly always depressed me anyway, and reminded me of my mother in her cocktail waitress days before she started working for the *Tribune*: the bottles of Crème de Menthe I used to find on the butcher's block when I came home from class; her boyfriends with their lame jokes and lamer attempts to ingratiate themselves—"Fetch me a Rob Roy, young man"; finding her passed out on the couch in the front room with the TV blaring; pouring all her liquor down the sink; feeling guilty for making her spend even more money on booze.

"Yeah," Conner said as we sat outside the brewery, listening to the muffled hollers of the football fans inside. "I don't have what I used to. I don't know how I lost it or where, and I'm not sure if I can ever get it back. Maybe authors shouldn't write more than one or two books. Maybe you just keep writing the same book over and over anyway. I've already written more than Salinger, Dudek, or Harper Lee ever did."

As the night wore on, people inside the brewery were still watching the game, but the Colts had fallen three touchdowns behind. Someone had turned down the volume and had turned up Dierks Bentley's "Lot of Leavin' Left to Do." The temperature on the patio was dropping fast, and Conner and I were the only ones outside. We asked our waitress, Abby, if she wanted to close out our tab.

"You can stay out here till my shift's over far as I'm concerned," she said, then added to Conner, "I'm a fan, hon. I loved that *Devil Shotgun*. Have you ever written anything else?"

Conner gave a somber half smile. "Yes and no," he said.

I left the table, ostensibly to use the john, but really so that Conner and Abby could continue their conversation. I didn't peg Conner for a guy who would pick up women on the road, but then again, I wasn't sure I would have resisted the temptation. Unfortunately, as far as I was concerned, the average age of my audience when *Nine Fathers* came out was about seventy-five, so I was never particularly well tested in this area. But when I came back from the Upland bathroom, Abby was gone and Conner was on the phone with Angie. Apparently, Angie had asked how many people had shown up to his reading.

"Not too many," he said, then quoted me: "It's kind of a sleepy little college town."

"Yeah," he added, he was off to Chicago in the morning and he expected a better turnout there. He told her he had run into "an old friend" but didn't mention my name. The time I met Angie while interviewing Conner in the Poconos, she seemed suspicious—answered questions tersely; kept eyeing my minidisc recorder, legal pad, and pen with a dour, judgmental expression. "She's just protecting me; she used to be a cop," Conner had said. "She knows that talking too much can get you in trouble."

I wondered if Conner remembered Angie hadn't liked me. Or

maybe he just figured she wouldn't remember who I was and didn't want to bother explaining.

"Kiss Atticus for me. I love you guys," he told her before he hung up, but from his expression, it seemed clear she hadn't said "I love you too."

"Marriage," he said with a wry, weary laugh. "It's a long, hard road, man."

With just about any other writer, I probably wouldn't have had the patience to listen to another tale of writer's block, of the difficulties of raising a family on mere advances, royalties, and film deals. "Get a real job," people in this town would have said, and though I would have taken umbrage if that statement had been directed toward me specifically, I would have probably agreed with the sentiment. When nearly 10 percent of the country was unemployed and foreclosures were at a record high, the fact that here in South Central Indiana, at the end of an all-expenses-paid book tour, a particular genre novelist was having trouble finding a topic to write about would have seemed low on the list of national tragedies. But Conner's chagrin seemed genuine, as did his concern for his family's future.

"I honestly don't know what I'm gonna do next, buddy," he said. "I started three books; I ditched all of 'em. I wrote a screenplay, a coupla pilots; no one bought 'em. My agent's frickin' eighty years old and she rarely takes my calls anymore—she's got her own personal shit to deal with, no point in me bugging her. Besides, I don't have a new book idea anyway. You know, me and Angie, we banked our futures on this career. It seemed like an easy bet to make, but man, it's just not payin' off."

Conner didn't mind the idea of going back to work at some newspaper job. If he and Angie economized, they could hire some help around the house. She could complete a master's in education at East Stroudsburg University, then get a job teaching kids, which was what she'd said she wanted to do when she quit the police force. Selling the Delaware Water Gap house and moving someplace smaller sounded fine to him. They didn't need a Porsche, either; it was a crappy car if you had a kid.

But Angie had gotten used to their lifestyle and was exhausted by the idea of starting over. They had felt elated when they learned she was going to have a child, but the pregnancy had been hard, and lately neither of them had been getting any sleep. They argued all the time, something they had never done before.

"I was hoping this book might change all that." Conner let his voice drift off; he didn't need to finish the sentence.

"I don't mean to lay all this on you, buddy," he said. "You're a good guy for listening and you've had more than enough of your own bullshit to deal with in your life. I'm amazed you can still hold it all together so well."

I told Conner all the stuff you're supposed to say, all those darkest-before-the-dawn clichés. I said he was a talented writer and that he would pull through and that all couples argued during that first year of parenthood, me and Sabine included. I told him just about every writer I had ever known wrote his best work when he had his back up against the wall and thought he would never write another word. And no matter how hackneyed and useless my advice seemed to me, Conner nodded and smiled ruefully, as if no one had ever given him such intelligent, sober counsel.

At the end of the evening, I drove him back to his hotel. We vowed to keep in better touch. We shook hands, hugged, and he repeated his invitation to Pennsylvania. I could bring Sabine and the kids and make a whole family weekend out of it, he said. "And better make it soon. Before we have to sell the house."

I wished him luck and said I trusted Chicago would be better than Bloomington.

"I sure hope you're right, man," he said.

I watched him stride toward the doors of the Indiana Memorial Union, then disappear into the lobby. I thought I'd probably never hear from him again, or if I did, it would be in another six or seven years after he had conquered his writers' block and written three more thrillers. Maybe by then Sabine would have tenure, and we'd have a bigger house in Walnut Creek, where the schools were better. I certainly didn't expect to hear from Conner the next night.

4

I didn't recognize the number when it appeared on my cell phone. I figured it was either a wrong number or someone from the Highway Patrolmen's Association Fund asking for dough. I was trying to fold laundry with one hand while using the other to keep Ramona from climbing onto the counter to take a pack of Gummi bears out of a cabinet—"No," I was saying. "You already had dessert. And you've already brushed teeth."

"I'll brush them again," Ramona said.

"Come on, stop it. Just get down from there."

Meanwhile, Sabine was trying to finish reading half a dozen papers for the panel she would be chairing at the American Political Science Association meeting while Beatrice was clinging to her leg. "Can you get her off me?" she asked.

I was going to let the call go straight to voice mail, but I noticed the Chicago area code. I had two immediate thoughts—either my mother was sick or Conner was calling. I picked up.

"Is this an OK time, buddy?" Conner asked. He sounded harried and out of breath.

"Not really," I said. "Can I call you back?"

"Yeah, sure, I guess." He hung up. I spent the next hour and a half reading *Island of the Blue Dolphins* to Ramona before she finally nodded off; meanwhile, Sabine fell asleep nursing Beatrice. I rinsed the rest of the dishes, put them in the dishwasher, turned it on, and finished folding the laundry. I put on a light fleece jacket, leashed my old border collie/husky mix Hal, then, when I got outside, I tried to call Conner back at the number he had called me from. Apparently, he had been calling from the Drake Hotel. I asked to be transferred to his room, but the desk clerk told me Conner wasn't in the "Author's Suite" anymore, and had said he would be checking out early.

"This wouldn't be Mr. Dunford, would it?" the desk clerk asked.

"Who?"

"Anyway, he's not here."

I took Hal to Bryan Park and back—didn't see a single human being on our entire walk. Then I went to bed, finding a slip of space next to my sleeping wife and our sprawled two-and-a-half-year-old. I had long passed my days of staying up late; I knew my kids would be up at six and wouldn't care whether I had gotten my seven hours. It was well past midnight when my Charles Mingus "Fables of Faubus" ringtone woke me.

"Hello?" I made my way out of our bedroom and into the darkened living room. I practically tripped over Hal, who growled slightly at my approach.

"Hey, man." Conner whispered loudly. "Did I wake you up?"

"Not at all. I was just doing some writing. What's going on?"

"I gotta talk to somebody," he said. "This is so messed up and I really don't know who else I can talk to about it."

"Sure," I said. "Shoot."

"No way. Not over the phone."

"OK." I waited for him to fill in the blanks, and when he didn't, I said, "You mean you want me to come all the way out to Chicago?"

"Nah, that's too far for you," he said. "And I need to get away from here anyway, to make sure no one's following me."

"Following you? What are you talking about?"

"I probably sound like I've been drinking, right?"

"Have you?"

"No. Look—can I borrow you tomorrow sometime during the day? Not for too long, maybe an hour or two? I know it's a huge favor to ask, but I can't call Ange. You're the one person I can call."

"Sure," I said. "Whatever you need."

"You're a bud," he said. "Hold on, let me look at my map." There was a half minute of silence, then Conner said, "Can you drive to West Lafayette first thing in the morning? There's a Hilton Garden Inn there."

"What's this all about?"

"Can't tell you now, man. Just need to bounce something off somebody. I'll tell you when you get here. You're a good listener; you like a good story, right? 'Cause this is a pretty good story so far."

"All right," I said. "I'll get there when I can."

"Can you try to make it by nine?"

"Do my best."

"And bring a bathing suit. They've got a pool. We might swim."

"What?"

32

"It'll all make sense when you get here, at least as much sense as any of it makes to me."

"OK."

"When you get here, ask for my room. I'll be staying under a different name."

"What name?"

"You should appreciate this, my friend." Conner laughed. "Salinger."

5

At this point, I should probably discuss my strange relationship with J. D. Salinger, which I really hadn't thought about all that much at the time, but it might clarify some events later on. When I was growing up on the north side of Chicago and attending high school at Lane Tech, where I pulled A's in English and D's in woodshop, a fair number of my friends were Salinger fans. In early December 1980, my best friend, Paul Benson—a guy I also lost track of shortly after I moved to Indiana—handed me his dog-eared, underlined copy of *Catcher* and told me to read it—"It'll rock your world, bro," he said.

I hadn't read Salinger before, but Paul and I were always trading books and we tended to trust each other's judgment. I gave him Kerouac and Burroughs; he gave me Vonnegut and Salinger. We liked Ayn Rand and William F. Buckley Jr., too, but let's not get into that—we were kids and it was a different era.

The night I cracked *Catcher*, I was sitting in the front room of the apartment where I lived with my mom. She was out, as usual, and I was alone watching *Monday Night Football* when Howard Cosell announced that John Lennon had been shot. I watched TV all night, listening to every update, finally learning that Lennon was dead, that his assassin's name was Mark David Chapman, and that Chapman had had a copy of *Catcher in the Rye* in his back pocket. Lennon was my favorite Beatle, and, just a few days earlier, I had read Aaron Gold's "Tower Ticker" gossip column in the *Chicago Tribune*, which reported that Lennon and Yoko Ono were considering playing the Uptown Theater to promote their new album, *Double Fantasy*. Sometimes, the *Tribune* gave free event tickets to its employees, and I had been planning to ask my mom if she could get me some. I wasn't so sure I wanted to read the novel anymore.

I was still debating reading the book a few months later when John Hinckley, another nut who liked *Catcher*, tried to assassinate Ronald Reagan. I learned about that in my debate class, when my teacher, Vicki Ryan, wheeled in a TV so we could watch the news. I vowed never to read Salinger's book. It was nearly a decade before I actually did read it. I was a fifth-year senior at the University of Illinois at Chicago, and I read the book on the 50 Bus, on rides between my apartment and campus.

Catcher made no great or lasting impression on me. It probably had too many negative associations for me to see its brilliance. It seemed like a manifesto for the antisocial, something I might have gotten more out of at age thirteen. I skipped the rest of Salinger's oeuvre.

Still, from time to time, whenever I saw Salinger's novels or story collections on my friends' bookshelves, or when I heard authors such as Conner talk about how much they admired the guy, I wondered how those books could have influenced them so greatly. I wondered too how Mr. Salinger—in seclusion for more than forty years in Cornish, New Hampshire—felt about the readers who admired his work. If somehow knowing he had touched Hinckley and Chapman had convinced him that escaping society had been the right move. I wondered how it would feel to write something—a story, a novel, an article—that would inspire someone to change his or her life for better or worse. In some small way, I got the chance to find out after I published *Nine Fathers*.

Though my book was a work of fiction, like all novels, particularly all first novels, it had its basis in autobiography. It was a satirical rendering of the life I had led as the son of a single mom, who kept just about all her past existence secret from me and who'd cut her ties with her previous life so resolutely that she never told me anything about my father, Sidney Joseph Langer, other than his name and that she met him at the Coq d'Or Lounge at the Drake Hotel, where she was working as a cocktail waitress. For all I knew, and for all the questions my mom left unanswered, she might well not have known any more about him than she told me. My "novel-in-stories" (that's what it said on the jacket) concerned a young man searching for his own identity and imagining nine different fathers he might have had. There was a rich father, a poor father, an artist, a criminal, a tinker, a tailor, a soldier, a sailor, and a spy. The book, which was told in nine different genres, was about the journeys I might have taken if I'd had a little more courage. I had often looked up old Sidney L. in phone books and in online directories and considered calling or visiting the people who had that name and lived at those addresses. But I never did.

The book was one I needed to write, but in retrospect, not one that anyone needed to read. I didn't think it would make much of an impression on my mother. She had often encouraged me to read, and kept numerous books on her shelves from her high school and college years—and like all Americans who came of age in the early 1960s, she kept some Salinger books in her collection. But I don't recall her reading much of anything aside from nature magazines and puzzle books. Plus, in *Nine Fathers*, though I'd used my father's real name in the hopes that he might happen upon it and find me, I'd described the character based on my mother as vaguely and sympathetically as possible. I'd changed all the biographical details, didn't mention her temper or her mood swings. I'd left out just about anything that would have led readers to believe she neglected me. I didn't mention her wealthy, cocktail-swilling boyfriends, most a minimum of ten years older than her. I didn't write about the packs of Virginia Slims she asked me to buy for her, about the spending sprees, the occasional shoplifting charge, or the Rob Roys or Crème de Menthe. I didn't even include the fact that her job at the *Tribune* consisted of writing the Anagrams and Jumble for the *Trib*'s puzzle page, which I thought would have struck readers as hackneyed symbolism even though it was actually true.

Shortly before it was published, I gave my mother a copy of *Nine Fathers*. By then, she had reached retirement age, but she was still working at the *Tribune*. When I would speak to her over the phone, I would wait for her to mention the book, but she never did, and I grew to suspect she hadn't read it, and probably never would.

But an interview I did with Steve Edwards, the host of a Chicago NPR show, caught her attention. Having written hundreds of author profiles, I understood the sorts of stories that captivated an interviewer. You were supposed to be snappy and glib, and you had to talk about how your writing was autobiographical, even, maybe especially, when it wasn't. And so I talked about my mother's secrecy and the mystery that constituted my father's life. I talked about the puzzles on the *Tribune* comics page and the Coq d'Or Lounge. I talked about the boyfriends Mom used to bring home—those silver-haired executives reeking of aftershave who ordered me to fetch ice for their cocktails and matches for their cigars, then offered me sips and puffs that I refused.

I didn't think I had said anything particularly offensive or controversial. But the day after the talk show, my mom sent me a stern e-mail: "You have sullied your parentage," she wrote. I tried to call her to get an explanation, but she never gave me one. For more than a year, she refused to take my calls. She didn't answer the e-mails I sent either. Only after Ramona, her first grandchild, started to speak full sentences did my mom begin to speak to me again, but our relationship had been irrevocably damaged. There had been a time when the two of us could talk for hours about anything; now, our conversations rarely lasted more than five minutes. I had written something that had wounded her and she could no longer trust me, she said. Mere words I had spoken had changed the trajectory of lives—mine, my mother's, and those of my wife and children. I began to sort of understand how it might have felt to be J. D. Salinger, how he might have been led to a life of seclusion. Once I'd had great plans for more novels, but after *Nine Fathers*, I weighed my words carefully and worried about the consequences of putting them into print. I had not completed another novel or story, and I was beginning to think I never would.

6

Room 110 at the West Lafayette Hilton was registered to a Mr. Jerome Salinger. It gave out onto Interstate 65, an unremarkable but functional highway that connected greater Chicagoland to Indianapolis. Conner had drawn the maroon curtains over his negligible view, their paisley pattern billowing stale gusts from the air conditioner, which was on full-blast even though, lately, Indiana mornings had been starting out cool.

Conner had moved the room's faux-mahogany desk and chairs away from the window, as if he were a spy afraid someone might see him through the window and try to assassinate him. He slapped me hard on the shoulder, thanked me for coming, and apologized for the "mysterious invitation." I noticed the beds were still made, and that Conner was wearing the same jacket, shirt, and jeans he'd worn at Borders.

"Yeah," he said, noticing what I was looking at. "Couldn't sleep, man. Didn't even try. You hungry?"

I shook my head. "Already ate."

"Coffee?"

"Water's good." I filled myself a glass from the bathroom sink.

"So," I said as I took a sip, "what do you need?"

"You bring a swimsuit?" he asked.

"Yeah, but I'm not much of a swimmer."

"Let's head down to the pool anyway," he said. "Might be safer."

"Safer?"

Conner assured me he wasn't worried for my safety, only his, and that the precautions were probably unnecessary anyway. He was just feeling paranoid that someone might have been listening to him or photographing him, and a swimming pool was more difficult to bug than a room. If he weren't married and if he didn't have a kid, he wouldn't have given a damn. But now safety was constantly on his mind. So I followed along with Conner's routine, which, if nothing else, was more interesting than my own. At this time of day, I would have been at home doing the diaper laundry, emptying the dishwasher, reading cookbooks, inspecting recipes on Epicurious, stalking old girlfriends on Facebook, and imagining other novels I could write that would probably get me into trouble—for example, *Nine Exes*.

Conner changed into a pair of black swim trunks; mine were orange and still a bit damp from the previous day at Bryan Park, where the kids and I had spent the day riding the water slides. We took the stairs down to the pool, which was empty save for a chain-smoking mom and her two boys who were eating Zagnut bars and littering the pool with their candy wrappers.

"You know, you're the only person I can tell this story to; you're the only person who'll *get* it." Conner took a sip of club soda and stepped into the pool.

I got in after him—the water was piss-warm and motionless. "All right, what's the story?" I asked.

"First, let me ask you something. Do you remember that book I told you to read when we were hangin' in the Pokes?"

I remembered. In fact, it surprised me that he remembered; I figured the time we spent together had made more of an impression on me than on him.

"Yeah," I told him. "We were talking about John Le Carré. *The Russia House*."

"That's right. There was a line in it I told you about. One of my favorites. You remember what it was?"

I didn't. In fact, I hadn't managed to read the book all the way through. I had always found Le Carré's books dense and slow-going, though I didn't mind some of the movies and BBC TV series based on his novels.

"That's all right," he said. "It's something the Russian agent says to Barley, the British publisher—'Promise me that if ever I find the courage to think like a hero, you will act like a merely decent human being.'"

Conner repeated those last five words. He lingered over their syllables as if they were part of some prayer he had learned back in Catholic school—*a merely decent human being*.

"I have a feeling this story may turn out to be kind of like that," he said.

"Why?" I asked. "Are you about to become a hero?"

"Not me," he said. "Maybe the opposite."

"You mean a villain?"

"Yeah," Conner said. "Maybe something like that."

41

7

The sun was beating down hard, and here we were—two forty-year-old guys in swimming trunks and baseball caps sipping club sodas in the shallow end of a pool at a roadside Hilton in West Lafayette with a view out onto the Interstate and the Flying J rest stop. I joked to Conner that we probably looked like a couple of kingpins planning a drug deal, but that was wishful thinking. I'm sure we looked more like a couple of washed-up dads waiting for our kids to come down to the pool. My baseball cap shaded my face, but I could still feel the sunlight reflecting off the water, charring my cheeks. Conner's skin was already bronzed, which pretty much summed up the differences between him and me—he tanned; I burned.

"How was Chicago?" I asked.

"Not all that great," he said. He had taken the first flight out of Indy, and arrived at ten in the morning at the Drake Hotel, where he checked into the Author's Suite, reputed to be the smallest suite in the hotel—even I had stayed in there when I was touring to support *Nine Fathers,* which should give you an idea of its modesty. He got a ride to Navy Pier, where he conducted an interview at WBEZ with the daytime host Rick Kogan, who had replaced Steve Edwards, the dude I held partially responsible for ruining my relationship with my mother.

Conner called Angie a couple of times to check in and see how she and Atticus were doing but, as always seemed to be the case these days, her temper was short and she seemed rushed; all she wanted to discuss was the work she needed to do around the house and what Conner would need to do when he got home—the toilet was backing up again; paint was chipping in the nursery and she sure hoped there wasn't lead in it; the seventh year on their adjustable rate mortgage was rapidly approaching. So Conner spent most of the day wandering along Lake Michigan, checking out the boats, the swimmers, the sunbathers, and the chess players, seeking inspiration for his next novel. Then he started heading north to his bookstore event.

"That's just about when things started getting weird," he said.

Conner's publisher had hired a driver to take him to his reading at the Borders on Clark Street and Diversey Avenue, about three miles from his hotel, but since he didn't have any plans, he'd decided to walk. The Chicago weather was oppressive, steamy; the bricks of air-conditioned buildings sweated out heat as Conner strode north on Clark Street, making his way past the singles' bars and restaurants of the near north side. He strolled by the tony homes of heirs and heiresses to industrial fortunes on the Gold Coast, then on through Lincoln Park, once home to David Mamet, Stuart Dybek, and a handful of other writers Conner admired. He took a shortcut through the Lincoln Park Zoo, where even the animals seemed to be having a hard time contending with the heat. Sad rhinos were gathered in small, muddy pools; the weary and somewhat mangy polar bear didn't seem to want to get out of the water; the gorillas were in a better mood—they had air conditioning.

Near the gift shop on his way out, Conner caught sight of a lone coyote that seemed almost to blend in with the slab of slate upon which he was standing. Conner spent some time staring into that animal's pale blue eyes. "You and me, man," Conner told that coyote. "You and me. We're just doing what we have to do to survive, and here we are, man, doin' it on our own."

When Conner got to Diversey Avenue, he started to feel more upbeat about his life. He was healthy, strong. He had a great wife, a beautiful son, both his parents were still alive. The streets and sidewalks were busy and the people on them seemed young, full of energy.

There was a line of people in front of the bookstore; the line was made up mostly of tweens with dyed hair accompanied by their parents and black-clad Goth kids on their own. Two news vans and a limo were parked in a loading zone, and a couple of bodyguards were standing by the front door, speaking furtively into their mouthpieces. Conner half convinced himself his interview on NPR had gone better than he had imagined and had generated this crowd. He also half convinced himself that Barack Obama was in town, perhaps visiting one of his major fund-raisers, Penny Pritzker, who lived in the area. Maybe the president and the Pritzkers were fans of his work and wanted their very own copies of *Ice Locker*. Only when he got to the front door did Conner realize he was at the wrong bookstore—this was not Borders; this was the Barnes & Noble across the street, a relic of the late 1990s and early 2000s, when people actually thought a neighborhood could support two big-box bookstores. The people outside the B&N were waiting to meet Margot Hetley, who would be reading from *The Fearsome Shallow:*

Wizard Vampire Chronicles #8, or WVCVIII, as fanboys and fangirls referred to it. Everybody in line had a copy of WVCVIII; no one was holding *Ice Locker*. Across the street at Borders, a sign in the window read CONNER JOYCE READING TONIGHT! but no one was waiting in line outside.

Inside Borders was a more depressingly familiar scene—rows of mostly unoccupied folding chairs upon a grim, gray carpet; stacks of hardcover Conner Joyce novels no one was waiting in line to buy; a disinterested store manager marking time before the store would close for good and she would get laid off. Yes, there was a better crowd than there had been at the Bloomington store—about fifteen or twenty, Conner estimated—but nothing that would make his next phone conversation with Angie go any better than the previous ones. Nevertheless, he tried to stay focused and positive. When he stood up in front of the audience and took his place at the podium, he performed his usual spiel. Afterward, he answered the usual questions—he said he did the same thing whether he was speaking before five people or five hundred, felt that each person deserved respect. Then he took out his Sharpie and sat down at the signing table.

The people who waited in a small line to talk to Conner after the reading were the typical amalgam of fans, writing students, and collectors, the latter of whom were hoping that someday Conner's books would be worth more than they were right now. He took his time signing; he had plenty of it. The only items left on his schedule were a ride to his hotel, sleep, then a six a.m. trip to the airport. He would catch his flight to LaGuardia. He would pick up his car and drive it back to the Pokes, where he would have a serious conversation with Angie about selling the house.

Conner capped his Sharpie and was getting ready to leave when he saw another man waiting for him to sign his book. He hadn't noticed the man during the reading, and felt fairly sure he must have shown up long after it had begun because, given his leathery face and imposing presence, he certainly would have remembered him.

"Was he anyone you recognized?" I asked.

"No," said Conner.

"Who was he?"

"He said his name was Pavel."

8

Pavel wore sunglasses. He was a bulky man in a mothballed tweed jacket, black shirt, and dark pants, all of which seemed a little tight for him, and he had a demeanor and sense of personal space that would have indicated he was Eastern European even before he opened his mouth and revealed his accent. Conner said he looked as if he might once have worked on a security detail for Vladimir Putin. He was hulking over the signing table, thumbing through a copy of *Ice Locker* when Conner caught his attention and asked if he wanted him to sign the book. The man nodded with a slightly sardonic smile that suggested a sly sense of humor at work beneath the thuggish presence, the bullish posture, and the shades. There was a bulge near one of his shoulders that made it look like he might have been carrying a weapon.

The man proffered his copy of *Ice Locker.* "If you *plizz*," he said.

Conner took the book from the man, who told him how much he had enjoyed it. Odd—the man didn't give off the impression of being much of a reader, and Conner was further surprised when he told him how accurate his novels always were, how much specific detail they provided about forensics and police procedures.

"You know my work," said Conner.

"I do."

"So," Conner asked. "Who should I make it out to? The signature?"

"Make it 'To Dex.'"

"Sure." Conner signed and dated the book, at which point Pavel slid a stack of about a dozen books across the table and placed them in front of Conner.

"All these too," Pavel said.

"Signatures on all of them?" Conner asked.

"Yes. And make them all 'To Dex,'" said Pavel.

"You must be quite a fan," said Conner.

"Dex is, yes."

Conner stopped in the act of signing. "You're not Dex?"

"That I am not. But he would like to meet you."

"Who? Dex? Is he here?" Conner continued to sign the books that Pavel was placing before him.

"No, but I can take you to him whenever you like."

"I don't think so, buddy; I don't swing that way," said Conner.

"Neither does Dex." Pavel took off his sunglasses and looked directly into Conner's eyes. The man reminded Conner of that coyote he had seen at the Lincoln Park Zoo—searching, scheming, alone.

"It would be worth your while. I guarantee this," Pavel said, and after Conner asked him what he meant, Pavel told him Dex wanted to make Conner "a sort of proposal."

48

The proposals Conner tended to get from strangers at readings were usually either bizarre or depressing, most often some combination of the two. Sometimes, a writer wanted Conner's opinion on a manuscript or a recommendation for an agent or editor. Once in a while, there was a woman, usually unhappily married—she would want to know how long Conner was staying in town and if he had time for a drink. Conner always kept his responses polite yet guarded. He gave the writers his agent's e-mail address and the name of his editor; he told the women he was busy and, if pressed further, married. The conversations usually ended there, but when Conner offered to give Pavel the name of his editor and publicist, Pavel said no, that wouldn't do.

"This proposal Dex has to make to you, he will do it in person," said Pavel.

Conner almost laughed out loud. He wondered whether Pavel's use of commanding phrases—you *will* do this; he *will* do that—was intended to sound as threatening as it did or if Pavel's English was just that lousy.

"Oh, he will, will he?" Conner asked.

"Yes, he will," Pavel said. "Tonight, in fact." And after Conner asked him what Dex's rush was, Pavel smiled slightly. "This is because you are leaving on the seven forty-five a.m. flight for LaGuardia, are you not? There would not be time tomorrow, would there?"

"Seven forty-five?" Conner's voice wavered.

"United Airlines, Flight 110, to be exact," said Pavel. "This is true, yes?"

Conner got up from the signing table and, as he did, Pavel added, "Or, Dex could meet you at your hotel. You're staying at the Drake, this is also true?" Conner said nothing. He maintained his silence when Pavel added that Dex would be happy to meet either in the hotel's Coq d'Or cocktail lounge or in the Palm Court.

"Or," Pavel added with a sly smile, "if you prefer, the two of you can meet in the Author's Suite, Room 813, is it not?"

"How do you know all that?" Conner asked, but before Pavel could respond, Conner decided he didn't want to hear the answer. He headed for the door. His Spidey sense was tingling big-time, he said. Conner reached the front door of Borders in time to hear Pavel tell the bookstore manager, "I will take the rest of these. And I would like to have them delivered to Six Hundred and Eighty North Lake Shore Drive." When Conner looked back, he saw that Pavel was buying every one of his books and taking out a phone to make a call.

9

Conner stepped out of Borders and flagged down a cab. He didn't have much of a plan in mind other than to return to his hotel, pick up his suitcase, and check out. He didn't understand how Pavel had known where he was staying and what his travel plans were. Maybe Pavel was a friend of his editor, or maybe he worked for a publisher from the former Eastern Bloc, one as yet unschooled in Western codes of conduct. But Conner didn't want to stick around to find out. When he had worked as a crime reporter, he had no fears of interviewing gangbangers, of flashing press credentials at the wardens of Rikers Island, of hanging around precinct station houses well past midnight, then walking all the way home—in fact, he had met Angie at the Twenty-Fourth Precinct headquarters on 100th Street, and they routinely walked home to her mother and aunt's apartment in Hamilton Heights, where she continued to live until she and Conner got married. But now that he was a husband and father, he preferred to let his characters take risks while he enjoyed cups of hot tea and mugs of home-brewed beer on the back deck of his house in the Pokes.

Traffic was heavy on Diversey Avenue. The Margot Hetley reading had just let out, and all the tweens and Goth kids who had been waiting for Hetley to sign books were pouring onto the streets; they were heading for the bus stops and elevated train stations, forming a flash mob as they threw "vampard" signs at one another and roughly shoved passersby while Hetley's limo sped away from the store. Conner exited Borders before Pavel, but by the time his taxi managed to make an illegal U-turn to start heading south toward his hotel, he could see that Pavel was getting into a cab too. At that moment, Conner felt an urge to say all the things detectives say to taxi drivers in other genre novelists' books, but rarely said in his own: "Step on it, Driver," and "Lose that tail." But he just gazed silently out the window at the boats on Lake Michigan, the cars speeding along Lake Shore Drive; he looked west toward the Lincoln Park Zoo—an immense black emptiness beyond the rippling Lincoln Park Lagoon; he could imagine that lone coyote howling upon his slab of gray rock. He looked through the back window of the cab, trying to see if he could spot Pavel's taxi, but there were at least a dozen cabs and it was impossible to say which one might have been his.

When Conner got back to the hotel, he greeted the doormen and security guards loudly—he wanted them to know who he was and to remember him in case anything happened to him. He had never had these sorts of morbid, nervous thoughts before he became a parent. He zipped up the blue-carpeted steps, taking them two at a time. He greeted businesspeople heading to the cocktail lounge, tourists clutching bags from the Apple Store, tuxedoed and evening-gowned couples en route to rehearsal dinners. At the hotel's front desk, he told the clerk, an officious young man of about twenty-five with a pencil-thin mustache, affecting some sort of English accent, that he wanted to check out early.

"Certainly, Mr. Joyce." The man typed on his computer to pull up Conner's bill. "Oh," he said. "Some men were looking for you before."

"Men?" Conner asked.

"Two of them. They left this." The man produced a note written on watermarked, ivory-laid stationery. On it, in exquisite handwriting: "Mr. Joyce, I'm downstairs at the Coq d'Or Lounge. Regards, Dex."

Conner gave the note back to the desk clerk. He passed the man a twenty-dollar bill, and asked him if he could arrange to have a bellhop take his suitcases down to the lobby.

"Are you sure there's nothing wrong?" the man asked. Conner looked down to the main entrance of the hotel and saw Pavel approaching the revolving doors. Conner headed downstairs. He made his way to the first door he could find, which led to the men's room.

Conner scrubbed his face, using a white washcloth from a small wicker basket by the sink. Was he overreacting? What was there to be frightened of? An Eastern European man had bought a bunch of his books and asked to introduce him to a friend. Sure, something about the man seemed sinister, but no one had threatened him. Perhaps this Pavel and his friend Dex, whom Conner imagined as a bald-pated Russian mobster who dabbled in the black market— maybe something to do with uranium rods—didn't understand that you didn't randomly approach authors, buy all their books, and demand special meetings. Perhaps Dex was just uncommonly rich and didn't think the usual protocols applied to him. Perhaps the usual protocols were stupid. Conner was continuing to work through scenarios when he looked in the mirror and saw the door to the bathroom opening. Pavel was entering.

To his left, Conner espied another door. On it was a brass plaque engraved, TO COQ D'OR LOUNGE. His face not yet dry, Conner made his way to that door and entered.

10

I knew the Coq d'Or well. When he was still alive, my father was a fan of the place—at least, that's what my mother told me. When he was in town on business, he drank there, entertained friends, and, on one fateful evening, met a young cocktail waitress and invited her up to his suite, where I was conceived. After I graduated college and moved out of my mom's apartment, I wrote short stories in the Coq d'Or, hoping to connect with some aspect of my past, but also because it was an atmospheric joint with excellent soups and the best club sandwich in Chicago. The waitstaff knew rich people tended to be eccentric; even if you dressed poorly and didn't look like you had much dough, they didn't hassle you about sticking around all night.

But to Conner, stepping into the Coq d'Or was like stepping into a world he had only read about in books, or perhaps seen in movies about ad execs in the early 1960s. The place was a piano bar populated largely by well-heeled, martini-swilling tourists and the occasional regular from Chicago's Gold Coast aristocracy, some of whom owned apartments in the Drake, many of whom were alcoholics; some of the men were accompanied by high-dollar escorts; some of them paid their bills with Drake Hotel credit cards, a perk offered to hotel regulars. There were white tablecloths, maroon leather booths, a long oaken bar behind which a white-clad bartender operated a cocktail shaker. In the air was the scent of lobster and clam chowder. On the night Conner entered the bar, a tuxedoed pianist was playing "Stardust" and doing a surprisingly good job of it. In another era, Conner would have expected to see women smoking long cigarettes and men puffing on stogies, but what Conner actually saw was a man he immediately knew was Dex Dunford.

"Was that his real name?" I asked Conner.

"I doubt it," he said.

The man was sitting alone at a table with copies of *Ice Locker*, *Devil Shotgun*, and Conner's other three novels placed atop it. Clad in a dark-blue, pinstriped suit with a pale-blue pocket square, he looked dapper, even debonair. As he sipped his Rob Roy dry on the rocks with a twist, he could have been nominated for "America's Best Dressed Executive" during a time when people were still nominated for such titles. Dex was a small man—slim, yet authoritative. His hair was full and white, and upon first viewing him, Conner couldn't decide whether he looked more like a fifty-year-old man from another decade or a well-preserved seventy-five from the present one. Propped up against the wall behind Dex was a hand-carved walking stick with the face of a yellow-eyed falcon for a handle.

"What would you care to drink, Mr. Joyce?" Dex asked. His accent sounded vaguely British, but that seemed more a function of class than geography; he spoke with what passed for a generic, wealthy cadence, favored by actors from the Golden Age of Hollywood, such as Clifton Webb or Ray Collins; he didn't pronounce the *r*'s at the ends of his words.

Conner didn't answer Dex's question. He wasn't sure he would be drinking anything at all.

"Please, sit," Dex said. "What harm could possibly come to you by merely sitting down for a drink?"

Conner didn't immediately answer. "Well, I suppose you're right, after all," said Dex. "Why, all sorts of harm could come to you. After all, we've never met. I do feel I know you, though, Mr. Joyce." He said he was a fan of Conner's work. He had read all the Cole Padgett books. He liked the new one, *Ice Locker*, he said, and thought it was one of Conner's better works. He said he always loved his attention to detail, the specificity of Conner's locations. "But it's hard for any writer to outdo his first success," Dex said.

Conner began to relax. He was familiar with this sort of conversation; it was the same sort he had with the people who attended his book readings or interviewed him on public radio shows.

"Are you in the business?" he asked.

"Which?"

"Publishing."

"Not exactly," Dex said. "I collect."

Conner took the seat across from Dex, and when a waiter asked if Conner would be eating or drinking anything, Conner agreed to take a glass of ice water.

"A collector," Conner said. "You mean first editions?"

"In a manner of speaking," said Dex. He asked Conner how *Ice*

Locker had been selling, and when Conner muttered something about how it was too early to know, Dex asked if the book was doing any better business than his last two novels had. Dex assured Conner that he wasn't trying to pry; he was genuinely concerned because he understood how hard it was for writers to maintain their careers.

"You shouldn't take it personally," Dex said. "My last two authors took it personally, even though I assured them they shouldn't."

"Authors?" Conner asked. "Didn't you say you didn't work in publishing?"

"That's true," said Dex. "I did say that, sir."

"What business are you in?"

"I believe we're getting ahead of ourselves." Dex motioned to the waiter and summoned another Rob Roy for himself.

Time passed, perhaps an hour. The pianist finished his set with a medley of Cole Porter tunes, then made his way to the bar, where a martini and a girlfriend in a black sequined gown awaited him. Men who had entered with escorts left with those escorts, presumably en route to one of the hotel suites that was far better appointed than the Author's Suite. Although Conner couldn't say he was beginning to feel comfortable around Dex, he did sense, as long as he remained in this bar, no harm would come to him. The rest of the evening seemed clear. Once he left the Coq d'Or, he would get his bags from the porter, grab a cab, and head to the Hilton at O'Hare.

When Dex was done with his third Rob Roy, he made a writing-in-the-air gesture to the waiter. He paid his tab, then put his palms down on the table.

"So, Mr. Joyce," he said. "Are you ready?"

"Ready for what?"

"For me to show you something," said Dex. "But I'm afraid that you'll have to come with me to see it."

Conner's Spidey sense began to tingle again. "Why can't you just tell me about it?" he asked.

"Because, my friend," said Dex, "you won't believe a word of what I tell you until I show you." He reached into an inside pocket of his suit jacket and withdrew an envelope.

11

The envelope was plain white. Inside were two items. The first was a calling card upon which was written in embossed gold script—*"Dex Dunford, Collector of First Editions, 680 N. Lake Shore Drive."* There was no phone number or e-mail address.

"This is you?" Conner asked.

"It is." Dex pointed to the address. "And that's where you and I will be going."

Conner took out the second item—a personal check made out to Conner Joyce for $10,000. The handwriting was loopy, exquisite, drawn with a fountain pen.

"And what's this supposed to be?" Conner asked.

"A down payment," said Dex.

"For what?"

"Nothing the least bit sordid, I can assure you. Nothing that would endanger or compromise you in the slightest. But again, before we reach my apartment, there is no point in telling you anything further, for I can assure you that you won't believe me."

"How am I supposed to know I'll make it back in one piece?" Conner asked.

"I would assume that my word as a gentleman would suffice," said Dex. "But since it rarely does these days, you may do this: Take note of the address on my calling card. You may leave the card with the desk clerk upstairs. Tell him if you're not back in ninety minutes to call the police and direct them to my address."

As for the check, Dex said he would advise Conner to keep it in his wallet. For, though he had dealt with this particular desk clerk many times over the years for transactions such as the one he would soon be proposing, ten thousand dollars posed too great a challenge to trust any man with.

"Apparently, you've plotted out everything," Conner said.

"I have," said Dex. "In fact, I've even thought of one other thing that might make you feel safer."

"What's that?"

Dex reached into his pocket, pulled out his phone, and touched the speed-dial icon.

"Pavel?" Dex said into the phone. "Please join us."

Dex pocketed the phone. "You've already met my bodyguard, yes?" he asked Conner.

"Why do you need a bodyguard?" Conner asked.

Dex smiled. "For a man of my wealth, lifestyle, and history the question should be, 'Why do you need only one?'"

Pavel entered the Coq d'Or, then sat at the only unoccupied seat at Conner and Dex's table. He reeked of cheap aftershave, the sort found on sale in jugs at airport duty-free shops. "Yes, Mr. Dunford?" Pavel asked with slight amusement. But he seemed to know why he had been called. He was already reaching inside his tight, tweed jacket when Dex told him, "Please give Mr. Joyce your gun."

"Of course." Pavel placed a snub-nosed .45 on the white tablecloth before him.

The piano was closed, but the pianist was still drinking at the bar with his sequined girlfriend; the bartender was polishing glasses with a rag; the waiters were gathered around the bar, watching a Formula 1 race on a mounted television; most of the tables were empty, and yet Conner was wondering who might be watching, who else might catch a glimpse of this gun. What had the gun been used for? he wondered. What would he risk by holding it? By putting his fingerprints on it?

Dex jutted his chin toward the weapon. "The characters in your books seem to know how to use one, but do you?" he asked.

"I do, actually."

"Well," said Dex, "then you will be able to tell from its weight that it is loaded. Now, put it in your pocket."

Conner weighed his suspicions against his curiosity. The offer of ten thousand dollars had the effect of overruling his suspicions. The money would come in handy, whatever Dex was planning. No matter what happened, when he arrived home and Angie asked how the tour had gone, he would have a story to tell and a check to deposit—if the check was good, of course.

Conner put the gun in a jacket pocket, and Dex handed him a black-and-gold fountain pen and a sheet of stationery with his Lake Shore Drive address embossed upon it.

"What's this for?" Conner asked.

"For the note you'll be leaving with the desk clerk. It's a good pen. You may keep it. When you return to the hotel in an hour and a half's time, you may keep the ten thousand dollars, regardless of whether you agree to my proposal or not. Are we ready?"

Dex and Pavel stood, then Conner followed suit. As the men exited the Coq d'Or where Dex had left a $50 tip on the table, Conner headed toward the blue-carpeted steps that led to the main lobby of the hotel while Dex and Pavel made their way to the front door. When Conner reached the desk clerk, he scribbled a note—"I will be traveling with Dex Dunford to 680 N. Lake Shore Drive. If I am not back in ninety minutes, call the police immediately, and send them to this address."

He handed the note to the desk clerk, then noticed a house phone on the desk in front of him. His own phone was almost out of juice, so he asked the clerk if he could make a call.

12

That was when I called you the first time last night, buddy," Conner told me.

Here by the Hilton pool in West Lafayette, Indiana, the temperature had already climbed ten degrees since we had arrived and we were reclining upon a pair of white, plastic lawn chairs, drinking Diet Pepsi. Conner was lying directly in the sunlight, while I lay in the shade cast by a gray Hilton umbrella that had once been white.

I felt somewhat sorry that I hadn't been able to talk to Conner the previous night, but I wasn't sure what useful advice I could have given him anyway. Never would I have joined some mysterious gentleman and his gun-toting Eastern European henchman on that fateful journey to 680 N. Lake Shore Drive. I'm not a risk-taker, would no more get in a car with a stranger at age forty than I would have at age four. At the same time, I had full confidence in Conner's ability to survive, and no matter what the danger, I knew I would have wanted to hear the story.

"Of course you went," I said to Conner.

"I did."

"So what happened?"

Conner said he was surprised by how empty the streets were when he joined Dex and Pavel, who were waiting for him in front of the Walton Street entrance of the Drake Hotel. He had always thought of Chicago as a smaller Manhattan, but it was actually far larger and more spread out. Chicago wasn't a city that never slept; it tended to go to bed around ten p.m. Outside, in the still-searing summer night—nights didn't cool down in Chicago the way they did in Indiana—every restaurant seemed closed; hotel lobbies were empty; sidewalks were populated by a smattering of nervous city dwellers walking home as quickly as they could and tourists who thought they were in a smaller New York and didn't realize they were supposed to move fast.

Conner looked for a car, imagining a sinister black Volga with a posse of arms dealers inside. But he didn't see any vehicle waiting.

"Where is it?" Conner asked. "The car."

Dex's face registered puzzlement and disapproval. "I wouldn't feel comfortable getting into a car with strangers, and I wouldn't expect you to do so either," he said. "No, we will walk. The air is good, the night is lovely, and we won't be walking far."

And so Conner strode between Pavel and Dex, heading east, passing darkened doorman buildings and restaurants that had shut down hours before. The only sounds Conner could hear were those of cars zooming down the Drive on their way home, the roiling black lake crashing against the shore, and the footsteps of these men—Dex, himself, and Pavel. Before them, the lights of the Ferris wheel on Navy Pier blinked on and off, like some electric god's eye.

"Tell me," Dex asked Conner as they walked, "how does it feel?"

"How does what feel?" Conner asked.

"The gun," said Dex. "To hold a weapon that so many others before you have held, so many notable individuals."

Conner snorted slightly. "Yeah? Like who else do you have in mind?"

"Well, Norman Mailer held that gun," Dex said. "Saul Bellow, also. He was quite old when he held it. His hands shook and I feared I might have to take it back from him, lest it go off inadvertently."

Conner followed the men as they turned south, passing stark, black apartment buildings—all bright emptiness in their lobbies, all darkness on the floors above. Dex continued enumerating the authors who had supposedly held the weapon Conner now had in his pocket. John Updike had held it, said Dex. And Jarosław Dudek. So had Robert Stone, Truman Capote, and even Harper Lee.

"You have to be joking," Conner said.

Dex stopped walking.

"Something you should know about me, Conner, if we are going to be doing business together," he said. "I appreciate a good sense of humor. I enjoy it on the rare occasions when I see it in your work. But I never tell jokes myself, and I never joke about business."

"I didn't realize we had decided to do business together," said Conner.

"We may not," said Dex. "That will be up to you."

Dex began walking again, propelling himself forward with his befalconed walking stick, and Conner and Pavel sped up to keep pace with him. Conner could now see the address up ahead for a high-rise apartment building—680 N. Lake Shore Drive.

13

I hadn't lived in Chicago for nearly fifteen years, had spent a little more than half that time working for *Lit* in New York and the other time keeping house in South Central Indiana, but I did remember 680 Lake Shore. It had once been the Furniture Mart and its original address was 666. The building's developers, fearing the satanic associations of 666 might scare off buyers, changed the address to 680. On the lobby floor when I lived in the city, there used to be a cocktail lounge called the Gold Star Sardine Bar, featuring cabaret singers, dishes of free cigarettes at every table, and, most important, no cover charge. It was reputed to be a good place to take a date, but not a date I was interested in seeing for more than one night; cocktail lounges with free smokes and cabaret tunes may have been my mom's favored venues when she was my age, but I didn't feel comfortable in them. During the few years when I was working at

CBS, writing radio news copy and fetching sandwiches from the White Hen Pantry for John Cody and the rest of the news reporters and anchors, I took interns and desk assistants from DePaul and Loyola to the Gold Star. I paid for their drinks, lit their cigarettes, then watched them go home with older, wealthier men. I never took Sabine; she would have found the place pompous and the music boring as hell.

Six-Eighty Lake Shore was the sort of building that was ubiquitous on the Upper East Side of Manhattan—uniformed doorman out front; marble floors and brass fixtures in the lobby; crystal chandeliers; a late-night, luxury grocery store on the first floor; a health club with splendid views of the city. But in Chicago, it was something of a rarity, a throwback to a previous age, like the Coq d'Or or Dex Dunford himself.

The doorman, in a dark-red jacket and pants with gold stripes and matching epaulets, was a short man in his early seventies with prominent front teeth. He greeted both Dex and Pavel—"Good evening, Mr. Dunford"; "Pleasure to see you again, Mr. Bilski." He had an understated, professional manner, which suggested a man capable of maintaining the confidences of tenants. But when Dex introduced Conner, using his full name, the man smiled broadly.

"Conner Joyce?" he asked. "The writer?"

The doorman told Conner how much he had enjoyed *Devil Shotgun*. "That was a seismic work, Mr. Joyce," he said. "Absolutely seismic. Did you ever write anything else?"

"I did and I didn't," Conner said, then followed Pavel and Dex into the lobby.

As the men approached the elevators, Conner watched himself in the walls of mirrors. To his surprise, his reflection portrayed a man a great deal more confident than he felt. He could see that he was taller than Dex, his body fitter and seemingly more agile than

Pavel's. As they rode the elevator to the penthouse, Conner tried not to feel tense—he reminded himself of the note he had left with the desk clerk at the Drake, of the gun he had in his pocket as he stepped out of the elevator and approached the door to Dex's apartment. He was leaving a trail. He had witnesses. In a book he might write, all this knowledge would have helped a character, given that character confidence, though it didn't do much for Conner himself—all he truly wanted was to return to his hotel, sleep, board his plane, then get back together with Angie and Atticus.

"So, what was Dex's place like?" I asked Conner.

"Lovely, and yet . . ."

"And yet what?"

"And yet it was so strange."

"Not what you expected?"

"Well, no," said Conner. "But at the same time it was exactly what I should have expected if I'd been paying attention. And, let me tell you something, my friend, what I found there—I think you're the one guy who would really appreciate this."

When they entered the apartment, Conner was taken with its elegance. He noted the Oriental carpets in the main room, the views that gave out onto Lake Michigan, but when he saw a small crater in the white wall of the main hallway, he stopped. The hole was about the circumference of a half-dollar and quite deep, revealing gray cement beneath chipped white plaster. Lines radiated out from the hole like legs from the body of a spider. Conner gripped the gun in his pocket.

"Ahh, I see you've found it," Dex said.

"Found what?" asked Conner.

"One of my most prized possessions. Do you know what it is?"

"A bullet hole."

"Exactly. Do you know who made it?"

Conner shook his head.

"Mailer," said Dex.

"Norman Mailer?"

Dex nodded. He said that the author had taken the very same walk that Conner had taken and the two of them had conducted a similar conversation. They had met in the cocktail lounge of the Drake Hotel. Dex had told Mailer he wanted to make him a proposal. He gave the man the gun and a check, then brought him here. But Mailer had not believed the gun was real. The moment they entered the apartment, he said, "Let's see what that baby's got," then fired the gun at the wall.

"It was then that he understood my story was real," said Dex. "This was years ago now, but I still don't have the heart to plaster over the hole."

Dex led Conner past the hallway and into the next room.

"My mind was going crazy," Conner told me. "I thought there might be a body. I thought there might be guns or a suitcase full of drug money, all this stupid shit. I didn't know what the hell there would be."

"So, what was there?" I asked.

"Books," Conner said.

14

"Dex had the most beautiful little private library I've ever seen," said Conner. "If I had the cash, I'd build myself one just like it."

"What was it like?" I asked.

"Shit, man. I'm not sure I can do it justice."

"Try."

In the center of the room was a long, lacquered ebony table illuminated by green glass desk lamps. Restored eighteenth-century reading chairs were adorned with golden filigree. Against one wall was a small wooden bookcase filled with manuscripts locked behind a plate of glass.

Conner stood in front of that locked bookcase, trying to determine what sort of manuscripts might have been inside when Dex produced a key, inserted it into the lock, and opened the bookcase's doors.

"Yes, you may look," Dex said.

Conner stepped closer.

Clearly, they were all original manuscripts—either written long-hand or typed on a manual typewriter. Many had apparently been written by famous authors, a good deal of whom were among Conner's favorites, some of whom he had written letters to when he was a young man. J. D. Salinger was one of the authors. So was Jarosław Dudek; there were manuscripts by Thomas Pynchon, Harper Lee, Margot Hetley, B. Traven, Truman Capote, and yes, Norman Mailer. Yet, Conner did not recognize any of the titles. All the manuscripts sounded like crime novels, though these authors were, for the most part, not known for crime fiction—Mailer's manuscript was *Mightier than the Gun*; Dudek's, *An Escape from Warsaw*; Salinger's was *The Missing Glass*. On each title page was a simple inscription, the one Conner Joyce had written on more than a dozen *Ice Locker* title pages—"To Dex."

As Dex stood behind him and Pavel lurked in the hallway, Conner stared at the manuscripts, trying to figure out what they might be. He took down the Mailer manuscript, opened it to a random page, glanced at it, put the manuscript back. Then he opened the Dudek. He thought he had read absolutely everything these men had written. But he knew he hadn't read these.

"Are they real?" he asked.

"How do you mean?" asked Dex.

"I haven't heard of any of these titles."

Dex took a seat at his table, his back framed by a view of Lake Shore Drive and the black lake beyond it.

"That's right," Dex said. "Some people collect art. Some collect autographs. I collect stories—novels, memoirs . . . if there's really any difference between them. It all depends upon the author's willingness and upon my fancy. As you may have noticed, my tastes tend towards crime stories. But you are absolutely correct—you won't find these in any other library in the world. You won't find them mentioned in any one of these authors' biographies, autobiographies, or bibliographies. The only place you will find them is here."

Conner selected another manuscript, this one by Margot Hetley—*Bluddy Brillyance: A Tale of Wizzerds, Vampyres, and Vampards.*

"Ahh, yes. Lady Hetley's book," said Dex. "No one knew her then. She'd written only one book, but I knew she had the gift. Ruthless. But brilliant. Pity I can't let you read it."

Dex returned the Hetley manuscript to the shelf. Conner turned his attention to *The Missing Glass.*

"But this one," said Conner. "Surely . . ."

"Surely what?" asked Dex.

"I thought he . . ."

Dex finished Conner's sentence for him. "Stopped publishing?" Conner nodded.

"Yes," said Dex. "In fact, he did. But that doesn't mean he stopped writing. You heard he wanted to stay out of the public eye? Well, that was part of our agreement as well. Still, everyone has his price. Even wealthy, reclusive authors. Every author you see represented here—they all made their agreements, and I paid each of their prices. All of this will be part of our agreement too, Conner—yours and mine, if you decide that you would like to work with me."

As Dex and Pavel both stared intently at Conner, the manuscripts in the bookcase began to make more sense. Apparently, Dex had commissioned these authors to write books for him. But what sort of books? And why hadn't he heard of any of them before? How valuable might these be if they were authentic? An original, unpublished novel by J. D. Salinger? One by Harper Lee? By Jarosław Dudek? Conner began reading the first page of the Salinger manuscript and instantly recognized his favorite author's style—it was like a fingerprint; you couldn't counterfeit it. But before he could get the slightest sense of the story, a shadow fell over the page, and he noticed Pavel standing beside him, holding open a hand. Conner looked over to Dex, who indicated to Conner with a slight jut of the chin that he should hand the manuscript back to Pavel. Conner did. Pavel reshelved the book. Dex stood and locked the bookcase. He placed the key in his pocket.

"That was another part of my agreement with these authors, and that will be part of ours, too," Dex said. He directed Conner to sit across from him at the library table. "No other readers aside from me." He looked up at Pavel, who was still guarding the bookcase. "Pavel may read, but no one else."

As Conner told me his story while we reclined on our poolside lounge chairs, I shifted back and forth between excitement and jealousy. I was fascinated by the idea of all these unknown works. Yet I was envious that Conner was, in a sense, being asked to join these men, while here I was in Indiana, once again listening to another author's story instead of telling my own. I was even more envious of the idea of writing a story, getting paid for it, and not having to share it with anyone or risk alienating anybody.

"I wish I could tell you more about the story in that Salinger book, buddy, or about any of the others. But they were all private books," said Conner. "He said he wanted me to write his very own private book."

You may wonder why I was so willing to believe Conner, why I accepted, almost without question, the idea that Conner Joyce, while on a book tour of the Midwestern United States, met a man who owned original manuscripts he had commissioned from J. D. Salinger, Jarosław Dudek, and all the rest, and asked Conner to join their ranks. But I am a generally believing sort. Perhaps this quality would make me a lousy juror, but at one time it had aided me greatly in writing author profiles. Authors liked telling me their stories because I listened, I didn't interrupt, and I believed. And even if I wouldn't believe any random mope who told me the story Conner Joyce was telling me, I certainly believed him—Conner was even more guileless than I was; I felt almost sure that he never lied.

"So," Conner said to Dex, piecing it all together, "you're asking me to write a book."

"That's it, exactly," said Dex. "A book for only one reader. Me."

"But why?" Conner asked.

"That's not so hard to figure out, is it?" asked Dex. "Isn't that what anyone with enough money would want?"

15

In that immaculate little chamber that resembled a reading room in one of the world's grandest libraries, Dex leaned forward in his chair and rested his hands upon the falcon atop his walking stick. He gazed at Conner and smiled.

"Tell me, Conner," he said, "who is your favorite author?"

Conner smiled wistfully, then looked back at the manuscripts Dex had shown him, now locked behind glass. "You've probably got half of them here," he said. "I used to write letters to some of them—Salinger, Pynchon, Dudek, Capote . . . all those guys."

"Letters," said Pavel. "I like this. This is quaint."

"Indeed," said Dex, then turned back to Conner. "Well, we all have our own fantasy about our favorite authors, don't we?"

"Which is what, exactly?" asked Conner.

"That the author is speaking only to us, that he is writing only for us, that no one on Earth has the same relationship to that author as we do. I have the same fantasy every time I read a book I love, no matter who wrote it, no matter when it was written. That the author has written his book only for me."

Conner considered. Well, yes, he had once had this fantasy too. As a boy, when he had read adventure tales by Rudyard Kipling and Robert Louis Stevenson; as a young adult when he had read *Catcher in the Rye*; as a grown-up reading Graham Greene and John Le Carré, he had wondered how any author had been able to capture his own thoughts so thoroughly—he, too, had fantasized that his favorite books had been written only for him. He had written something much like this in the letters he sent to Salinger, Dudek, Capote, and Harper Lee—letters that were never answered. And yet, wasn't the terrific thing about stories the fact that they joined readers together, that they made people realize they were not alone in their hopes, dreams, and fears? And, putting such philosophical questions aside, there was still the question of money. Writing was a business, and you couldn't expect to make a living writing books for only one reader. But before he voiced this concern, Dex said, "I wouldn't worry about how much money you'd get."

"Why?" Conner asked. "How much do you pay for this sort of thing?"

Dex gestured to Pavel, who reached into his jacket pocket and produced a few stapled pages that had been folded in three. Pavel approached the table and handed those pages to Dex.

"What're those?" Conner asked.

"Your contracts and royalty statements." Dex said that he and Pavel had calculated the amount of money Conner had netted over the course of his five-book career, taking into account agency fees, taxes, and the like, to be approximately $1.25 million.

It was an impressive-sounding sum, and yet for the decade of work that Conner had put into his writing career, it was not as impressive as he figured it should have been. Divided over ten years, adding expenses and health insurance after Angie had left the NYPD, the sum roughly equaled Conner's father's annual salary before he retired from his position as a fire captain, or perhaps the salary of a tenured associate professor at my wife's university, but without the benefits and pension plan.

"Would you say that amount's about right?" Dex asked.

Conner did some quick calculations in his head. "Give or take," he said. "I'd have to get home and go to my desk and look."

"We've already checked this thoroughly, Conner," he said. "But just so you don't think we're trying to take advantage of you by making you arrive at a quick decision, why don't we double that number?"

"Double $1.25 million?" Conner asked.

"Yes," said Dex. "Which would put our offer at $2.5 million."

Conner's jaw did not drop, he did not gulp, his heart did not race, his cheeks did not flush, and neither did he have any of the reactions a character in one of his books might have had. He couldn't imagine the offer was real, any more than he could imagine Dex's manuscripts were real. And yet this apartment certainly seemed to belong to someone who had that kind of money, and yes, even if he couldn't say with certainty that the manuscript he had browsed was actually the work of J. D. Salinger, it did seem to read exactly like something the man would have written.

Conner couldn't say anything except to repeat the sum Dex had offered. "Two and a half million. You're being straight up."

"Yes," said Dex. "You will receive one-third upon signing the agreement, one-third upon delivery of the manuscript, and one-third upon my acceptance of it."

"Acceptance based on what?" Conner asked.

"Based on whether the book meets my—shall we say, artistic—standards," said Dex. "Isn't that the same sort of arrangement you have with your own publisher?"

"It is," said Conner.

Dex walked over to an antique rolltop desk, unlocked it with a skeleton key, and slid it open. On the desk was another personal check. Dex took the check, brought it back over to the table, then placed it in front of Conner. The check was made out to Conner Joyce for the sum of $833,333.33. On the memo line, Dex had written "Upon Signing" in the same ornate, loopy handwriting as on the $10,000 check in Conner's wallet.

Conner had never thought himself a person who cared particularly about money, and yet when he thought about the security this sum could bring, when he thought about how one day it could pay for Atticus's college education, how he and Angie could pay off their mortgage, how they could stop arguing about whether to sell their home, he couldn't help but hope the check was as real as the manuscripts in the bookcase seemed.

"Where does your money come from?" Conner asked.

Dex's smile contracted. "What difference could the answer to that question possibly make to you?" he asked.

"It seems like the sort of information I'd have the right to know," said Conner.

"Why would it?" asked Dex. "Do you have any idea who buys your books? When you meet your readers, do you ask them what they do for a living? They pay $24.95 for your books; do you ask where that $24.95 comes from? Do you have a 'right' to know that?"

"Of course not," Conner said. "But we're talking about a whole lot more than twenty-five bucks."

"The principle remains the same," said Dex.

Conner had no argument for Dex. He had no idea who bought

his books, how they acquired the money to buy them. Perhaps they were saints, perhaps they were criminals; he never asked—come to think of it, it wasn't his business, no more than it's any of my business who you are or how you make your money. A few years earlier, Conner had gotten some flak because a scene in *Devil Shotgun* had supposedly inspired a bank robbery in Trenton, New Jersey. Conner gave no credence to that rumor. He had written a book; someone had committed a crime—there was no connection. Had J. D. Salinger known who John Hinckley and Mark David Chapman were before they bought his books or took them out of the library? Would it have mattered if he had? Had he returned the royalties he received from those purchases?

"Come now," Dex told Conner. "There is nothing mysterious here. Everything is exactly as it appears. Maybe even too much so. I have told you I am a fan of your work. I have said that your work inspires me. I have asked you to write a book for me. I have explained why."

"So," Conner said. "What sort of book am I supposed to write?"

Dex looked to Pavel. "Show Mr. Joyce the contracts," he said.

16

The Hilton pool had gotten too crowded. A busload of college boys wearing Valparaiso University gear were horsing around and swearing. Conner and I headed back to Jerome Salinger's room, where we toweled off, showered, dressed, and sat at the desk he had wedged between the two beds. On the table, Conner had placed the checks Dex had given him—the address was 680 N. Lake Shore Drive; the amounts were for $10,000 and $833,333.33. I could see Dex's loopy, old-style handwriting.

I imagined I would have felt far more nervous than Conner in the presence of the mysterious Dex Dunford and the hulking Pavel Bilski, and yet I wondered if the arrangement Dex had proposed wasn't where literature was heading anyway. Book sales were plummeting, publishers and editors were losing their jobs, pleasure reading was becoming an increasingly rare pastime, authors were forced to devise increasingly creative means to make their living. Maybe this was the future—writers being paid to create books for only one reader who would measure his status on the basis of which author he had paid to write a book solely for him. Fewer readers, but richer readers. Donald Trump would commission the next Joyce Carol Oates novel; Warren Buffett would pay Don DeLillo to write his memoirs; Jarosław Dudek, Harper Lee, Conner Joyce, and whoever else would write whatever book Dex requested, and he would place it in his private library where no one but he and Pavel Bilski would ever read it. I didn't know who would commission me to write his personal, private book—maybe my usual burrito maker at the Laughing Planet; maybe the tamale chef at Feast or the beer sommelier at the Uptown Café; maybe I'd have to pay myself—the ultimate vanity publication. Or I could live like one of those farmers paid by the government *not* to farm, and convince my mother and anyone else I might conceivably libel to pay me not to write my next novel.

Maybe there wasn't much difference between writing for one reader and writing for thousands. In a previous life, when I wasn't rewriting wire copy for radio or going to class at UIC, I used to make extra money performing stand-up comedy in sleazy little clubs in Lyons and Rosemont, Illinois—clubs with names like the Comedy Womb and the Last Laugh. I remember one night when I was standing before a crowd of about twenty drunk, hostile spectators. All of them were glaring at me as I performed my act, save for one big bearded guy in the first row who smiled and laughed the whole time. I never met that smiling big guy, but he made my entire evening worthwhile, made me feel as if I were connecting with one human being. Maybe the idea of trying to write for the masses was foolish and egotistical; maybe all that mattered was communing with one other human being. Maybe one smiling big guy was all any writer or performer ever needed. Maybe one Dex Dunford was as good as one million readers.

"So," I asked Conner, "did you sign the contract?"

"Not yet," he said. "I wanted to ask a friend's advice. The only one I could think of was you."

"Why me?" I asked.

"Don't be modest," he said.

"Believe me, I'm not."

"Don't be naïve, either."

"I'm not trying to be," I said. "Anyway, what's it like?"

"The contract? I can't find anything wrong with it. Take a look."

I stared at the contract just as Conner had stared at it in Dex's apartment, hoping and despairing, fretting and dreaming. Pavel showed him the documents the other authors had signed—Salinger's contract, Mailer's, Hetley's, Capote's, and Dudek's—all more or less the same as Conner's with perhaps a modification here or there. Sitting at that desk with a view out onto Lake Shore Drive and Lake Michigan beyond it, Conner asked Dex what sort of book he was supposed to write. He expected Dex to issue strict parameters that would make writing the book difficult, if not impossible. But the assignment was vague. Dex said he liked crime stories, particularly the sort that Conner wrote—dutifully researched, exceedingly detailed. He said he wanted Conner to write as attentively as he always did. He wanted an original crime story, an idea neither of them had ever read before. He preferred for Conner not to write another Cole Padgett thriller, but said he wouldn't put that stipulation in writing; he just thought writing something different would be liberating for Conner. Conner kept asking Dex specific questions while Dex responded with more vague answers. When Conner pressed further, Dex finally said he wasn't a writer, but if Conner really wanted an idea, why didn't he try this one?

"Just in case I lose all my money someday and I have to try to make it all back, why don't you write a book about a man who loses $2.5 million and finds a very original way to steal that very amount," he said. "I would like to see what you would do in a book about that."

That's what Dex had told Conner. But the contract itself didn't say anything about subject matter. It only stated that Conner would write a novel of a typical length and that Dex would pay him in three installments. There were a few peculiar items, but none of them seemed like deal-breakers. For example, Dex insisted that Conner write the book either longhand or on a manual typewriter. Conner was not to make any Xerox copies or carbons of any pages he wrote. If he took any notes, they were to be shredded or burned. Ditto for any drafts, which were to be kept in a locked drawer to which only Conner would have a key. Attached to the contract was a confidentiality agreement, stating that, once Conner had signed, he wouldn't discuss the book with anyone other than Dex, Pavel, or any of the authors who had previously written for Dex. But there was little danger of that happening—Norman Mailer wouldn't rise from the grave to debate the fine points of the contract. Since Conner hadn't yet signed the contract and wasn't bound by its terms, he apparently felt he wasn't obligated to keep the matter secret from me. Still, given that we were meeting at the West Lafayette Hilton, he didn't seem to be taking too many chances.

"I should probably have my agent look at this. Or my lawyer," Conner told Dex.

"No agents, no lawyers," Dex said. "This agreement is between you and me only. If you reveal a word about our agreement to anyone other than the individuals enumerated in it, this contract will be null and void, and all the money I pay to you will have to be returned to me. Do you understand?"

Conner said he did, but added that he would probably have to discuss the matter with his wife at some point.

"Not with your wife," said Dex. "Not even with your son."

Conner laughed. "My son is only one year old, man."

"One year and three months," Dex corrected. "But you are not to discuss this assignment with him, either. Not when he's one and not when he's twenty-one. If you discuss it with him *at any time*, you must repay the money I have paid you."

"But how would you even know whether or not I had discussed it with him?" Conner asked.

Dex said nothing.

"What would you do?" asked Conner. "Bug me? Bug my house? Tap my phone?"

"Would you really risk two and a half million dollars to find out?" asked Dex.

"I guess not," Conner said. "So, when would I start?"

"The day my checks have cleared." Dex looked at his watch. "You should probably head back to your hotel, so they don't think anything has happened to you. I'll expect the contract back by the end of the week."

"And when I finish the book—" Conner began.

"Don't concern yourself with that," said Dex. "I'll know how to find you." He extended a hand and Conner shook it. "I do so look forward to doing business with you."

Conner took the contract and the Montblanc pen with him as well as the checks. He gave the gun back to Pavel, who offered to walk Conner home; Conner demurred. He took a cab back to his hotel, and when he was in the Author's Suite, he called me and asked if I would meet him the following morning in West Lafayette.

Now, as he sat across from me in the Hilton, he asked, "So, what do you think, pal? You think I should do it, don't you?"

"Why're you asking me?" I asked.

"I told you. You're the only one who'd *get it*," he said. "You think I should do it, right?"

"I don't see how you could say no," I said.

"Yeah," he said. "I don't see how I could either."

Conner uncapped his fountain pen and signed the contract.

"Nice pen," I said.

Conner smiled. "Used to be Salinger's," he said.

II:
Upon
Submission

One day, I thought I was looking through a window. The next day, I thought I was looking in a mirror. This morning I realized there's no difference between the two.

Conner Joyce, *The Embargoed Manuscript*

17

I watched Conner sign the contract. Later, when he got back to his home in the Poconos, he would endorse Dex's checks and return the signed contract. The checks would clear, and more than three-quarters of a million dollars would appear in Conner's account. He would keep quiet about the agreement he had made with Dex, wouldn't even discuss it with Angie. He would tell her some story about how he had gotten the money. Even when he was rocking his son to sleep or jabbering to the child about this or that, he would make certain not to mention anything about the project he was working on. He didn't really think Dex and Pavel could eavesdrop on conversations he might have with a one-year-old boy. But at the same time, he knew Dex was right—it wasn't worth risking $2.5 million to find out.

I didn't learn about any of this at first, although, on a few occasions, Conner tried to make contact with me, phantom calls I didn't answer because I didn't recognize the number or because I didn't have time to speak with him and was too preoccupied to call him back.

By this time, I had my own concerns to worry about. The idea of the consequences a piece of writing could have on a person's life had become an all too pressing and personal issue for me, more so even than when I had published *Nine Fathers* and lost my mother's trust forever.

This isn't really my story, at least not yet. So, I won't bother you with all the details about what happened that changed my wife's and my secure lifestyle. Also, since I'm legally prevented from discussing some of these matters in detail, I could be putting both Sabine and myself in further danger by writing about it in more than the broadest of terms. Suffice it to say that there was a regime change at the Graduate School of Foreign Policy. Sabine's hang-loose, pot-smoking, reggae-playing department chair, Joel "Spag" Getty, who once told Sabine she reminded him of Uma Thurman in *Pulp Fiction* and said he would "shepherd" her through the tenure process, managed to get himself a better gig at Princeton. Rumor had it that he had become a hot commodity in the academic world, not because of his scholarship but because of the hot-tub parties he hosted in his Deer Park manse along with the other members of his band, the Rastabators.

Shortly after Getty announced his imminent departure, he was replaced as chairman by one of his colleagues, a slick number cruncher named Dr. Lloyd Agger, a product of Midwestern schools who had his eyes focused not only on the chairmanship of Sabine's department but also on a position high up in university administration. Since I still don't know the differences among a provost, a chancellor, and a dean, I can't say with certainty which position Dr. Agger coveted, but whichever it was, he apparently felt that making tough decisions, such as recommending cuts in his department, would make him appear to be a man who was not afraid to make deep sacrifices to maintain the bottom line. It was my wife's and my misfortune that Dr. Agger was elected to the chairmanship during the same year Sabine was going up for tenure. It was also our misfortune that when Sabine had her creaky Dell office computer replaced, she didn't think to wipe clean its hard drive. Somehow, one of Dr. Agger's henchmen, a busybody named Duncan Gerlach from the Informatics Department, discovered all the blog entries Sabine and I had written under the name Buck Floomington.

In the grand scheme of things, writing puerile remarks about colleagues' sexual proclivities, professional indiscretions, weapons collections, and poor hygiene habits might not have ranked high on the list of potential misdeeds for an employee. Surely, it didn't compare with, say, dating students or stalking them when they worked the register at Bloomingfoods natural grocery, or only giving teaching assistantships in exchange for hummers performed on moonless nights in the clearing in the IU woods known as Herman's Hideaway. *Allegedly.* Still, writing these blog posts on the office computer was probably not the smartest thing for a Columbia University PhD and her trailing-spouse husband to do. And even so, all this might not have posed such a great problem had Duncan Gerlach not sent copies of our blog entries to each member of the personnel committee shortly before they met to discuss my wife's tenure case.

Perhaps at a later date, perhaps after the statute of limitations has passed or the confidentiality agreement has expired, or perhaps when I decide to write at length about my own experiences and not Conner's, I could go into greater detail about all the letters and character references Sabine and I had to solicit for her appeal. Perhaps then I could talk more about the sudden stress we were feeling now that we knew staying in this town was far from a sure thing. Perhaps then I could talk about Ramona's insomnia, or Beatrice's fits of rage, or our dog Hal's new allergies.

Before I learned anything further about Conner, a rough autumn and an even rougher winter passed. We were still waiting for the university to weigh in with a ruling about Sabine's appeal. Sabine, a doggedly determined pragmatist if ever there was one, was becoming increasingly morose. She and I would stay up with Ramona and Beatrice until ten or ten thirty before we would talk and hash out what we would do if we had to move. Academic departments weren't hiring, and even if they were, whom could we get to write recommendations on Sabine's behalf? Dr. Ellsworth Crocker, whom I had nicknamed "The Retired COINTELPRO Mole" in one blog entry? Dr. Baynard Ruttu, who was so obsessive-compulsive he wrapped the SFP toilets in cling wrap whenever he used them, but did not remove the pee-splattered plastic upon exiting the bathroom? As for me, I was more than willing to work full-time, but journalism and publishing were dying, and who wanted to hire a one-book author with a résumé and Rolodex more than five years out of date?

Sabine's and my conversations were frustratingly circular. Though each night we vowed to get more rest, invariably one or both kids would awaken at six and we'd be back at the coffeemaker, rubbing the sleep out of our eyes, waiting to get the kids to school and day care before we'd go back to polishing our résumés and packing clothes and furniture to give to Goodwill.

To deal with all the stress and uncertainty, I had been taking Hal out for unusually long morning walks. Sometimes we'd drive out to Nashville, Indiana, where we'd hike along the trails of Yellowwood Forest, sidestepping shotgun shells. Or I would drive twenty miles out of town to Spencer, and Hal would join me as I looked for salamanders and bluebirds in Hoot Woods and by McCormick's

Creek. Lately, we had been exploring the trails that circled Griffy Lake, a man-made reservoir that was good for perch fishing. The trails I chose weren't particularly strenuous, but they were scenic and leaf-strewn, and when Hal and I walked upon them, time seemed to stop. There were raccoons, foxes, and families of deer; every so often, I would happen upon a crinoid or some other fossil that I could bring home to Ramona for her geology collection. And since I was usually the only hiker on these trails during work hours, I could spend as long as I wanted brushing Hal's fur on a bench without being disturbed.

One morning, I was driving our Volvo station wagon along the I-46 Bypass heading toward Griffy Lake when I noticed a silver Nissan Sentra in my rearview mirror. The bypass was a well-traveled road, and the Nissan wasn't an unusual car—but it was following too closely and I had to take the curves and hills quickly, for fear of getting rear-ended. When I pulled into the trailhead lot and found a space, the Nissan pulled in beside me. Conner was at the wheel. He had a few days' growth of beard and was wearing sunglasses, blue jeans, and a faded maroon Philadelphia Phillies T-shirt. He looked skinnier, and somehow menacing. As Conner got out of the car and approached, Hal pawed the back window of my car and howled. At first, I didn't even recognize him. I figured he was either some hippie who wanted to sell me nonpasteurized milk, or a tweaker hawking meth.

Conner took off his sunglasses and gave me a weary, dimpled smile. "Sorry to sneak up on you like that, buddy, but you're a hard guy to track down." He leaned in through my window. A few caresses and a scratch behind the ears, and Hal stopped barking. I should have expected Conner would be good with dogs.

"What are you doing here?" I asked.

"Looking for you, man," he said. I hadn't answered his calls and he hadn't wanted to bother me at home with my wife and kids around. He said he had driven by my house a couple of times and, when he saw me leave and I had finished dropping off my kids at school and day care, he followed me to the nature preserve.

"That's a little creepy," I said.

"Yeah, I know," said Conner. "Sorry about that."

"It's OK. You want to join Hal and me for a hike?"

"Sure," he said. That way he could look down from the path to make sure no one was following him.

"Who's following you?" I asked. "That Dex Dunford guy?"

"Or Pavel," he said. "Probably nobody, probably it's OK, but who knows—I don't feel sure about anything anymore."

18

Usually, when I was walking Hal, I chose the easiest hiking trails, the ones with lots of benches for rest, contemplation, occasional dog grooming, and all-too-frequent self-assessment, a practice that lately hadn't been leading anywhere useful. Here I was in a nowhere town with one book and two kids and a life story that was interesting only because I didn't really know the details of it. The stories in *Nine Fathers* were fairly dull in and of themselves; what made each story interesting to me was the fact that it could have been true.

Still, having grown up as the only child of a single mom who rarely ever came home before ten at night, I cherished my admittedly boring family life—a house, a wife, two kids, and a dog in south central Indiana. But I had never really thought too hard about what it would take to maintain that life. Lately, whenever I tried to justify my existence, Jack Lemmon squared off poorly against

Alec Baldwin in the *Glengarry Glen Ross* of my mind—*"Good father? Family man? Fuck you. Go home and play with your kids."* Still, my harsh judgment of myself hadn't yet led me to change my habits, hadn't led me to, say, finish writing a story for once, or opt for a "rugged" instead of an "easy" or "moderate" trail.

But with Conner there, I felt self-conscious about my lack of athleticism, and so I opted for the moderate-to-difficult Overlook Trail, which wound upward along a steep and rocky path, then snaked over the sprawling roots of oak trees before ending at a muddy bluff that looked out over the narrow, gray lake and the fishing boats upon it. The walk was challenging, but as long as I could hang on to the dog's leash and the strong animal could help pull me over some of the steeper turns, I felt steady. Occasionally, Conner asked if I needed a hand or if I wanted to rest for a bit, and even though I did, I said of course not; I walked these trails all the time.

"I hope I'm not flattering myself too much, and I don't want you to take this the wrong way, buddy," Conner said once we had reached the highest point of the trail. "But the more I think about it, the more I think you and I have a lot in common."

"How do you mean?"

"You know I feel a kinship with you," he said. "You're like the only person I can talk to and trust. I realize that now."

"Thanks," I said, though I didn't really understand why that was. Probably because I had written a flattering article about him.

"So you flew in all the way from Pennsylvania to see me and tell me that?"

"Nah," he said, "I had to fly into Chicago again; you're sort of on my way home."

"You saw Dex?" I asked.

"Yup."

"You write that book for him?"

"In a way."

"Everything go OK?"

Conner choked out a bitter laugh. "I wouldn't say that." He stopped walking for a few moments. He rubbed his face until his cheeks turned bright red under his beard. "Goddamn, man," he said. *"Goddamn."*

Conner was looking a little shaky, and sat down on the warped, rickety bench. I sat beside him.

"Well," I said, "at least you can feel safe that no one's following us or listening to us all the way up here."

"You can never be sure, ever," said Conner. "I know that now, my friend."

"Then are you sure you wanna be telling me about everything?" I asked. "Won't Dex make you give back all the money if he finds out you told me? Wasn't that what he said?"

"It's different with you," he said.

"Why?"

"Trust me. It is," said Conner.

And so, there on that hill in Bloomington, Indiana, beneath the graying skies that seemed to mirror the lake below, Conner started to tell me everything that had happened from the moment I last saw him in West Lafayette. Or, at least, all that he wanted me to know.

19

The story began a few hours after we had said good-bye at the Hilton Garden Inn. I had driven home to Bloomington, while he took I-65 to the Indianapolis Airport. By the time he got there, he had decided to take Dex's story at face value. He would do what Dex asked. If the check turned out to be good, he would take the money, write the book as well as he could, and feel blessed that this strange project had fallen into his lap. If it had been good enough for the other authors Dex had employed, it would be good enough for Conner. It was about time his luck turned around.

Back at LaGuardia, he got his car and drove to the Poconos. He felt energized by the prospect of devising story ideas. He hadn't felt so upbeat since he had first met Angela and they had talked about books and she had told him how much she hated contemporary crime novels because they were so implausible, and he had vowed he would write one she could believe was true. He had dedicated that novel, *Devil Shotgun*, to her, had even named it after the brand of exhaust pipe on her Suzuki motorcycle. How thrilled he had felt during those days, typing until dawn while she slept in his bed until it was time for her to get up and get ready for her shift.

Back then, writing hadn't been about making money or trying to appeal to a big audience. It hadn't been about trying to make back the advances he had been paid. The reason he wrote was to forge a deeper relationship with the woman he loved and wanted to marry. Although he had fantasized about publishing a novel at some point, he hadn't thought *Devil Shotgun* would be the one, not until Angela read it and told him it was too good to share with only one person, even if that person was the one who had accepted Conner's proposal to marry her. Everything that came afterward—the agent Conner secured to sell the work; the contract he signed with Shascha's imprint at Schreiber & Sons; the movie deal; the deals for all the Cole Padgett books that followed; the ability to quit his job at the *Daily News*, buy a Porsche 911 and a sprawling 1920s home built on four acres of land with great views, lousy plumbing, and a private path that led down to the Delaware River—all that had been extra. And none of it would have mattered had Angela not fallen in love with him, married him, and agreed to move with him to Pennsylvania and start a family. Even now, he would have given back every word he had ever put down on paper if he could have recaptured the joy he had felt during his first years with Angie.

Angela De La Roja was Conner's inspiration and had been for every book he had written. He had been attracted not only by her beauty, but also by her honesty. "Sometimes, I feel we're the only two honest people left in the world," he once told her. When he had talked to her as a beat reporter, he was stunned by all the confidential information she provided him, all the background details no other cop had ever given up. And he knew she didn't tell him all this to impress him or to make her bosses or coworkers look bad, but because she was incapable of lying and because she thought he was the only trustworthy journalist she had ever met; journalism was a profession she viewed with as much skepticism as she viewed police work, which was probably why she had seemed so suspicious of me. She had been hurt badly in her life—when she was twelve, her father had died in prison after having supposedly been set up to take the fall for a drug deal he'd had nothing to do with. Becoming a cop had been Angela's form of mourning and vengeance for the lies that had shattered her father's life; she had no time or patience for dishonesty. When a couple of cops she knew had been cleared of police brutality charges for beating confessions out of teenage suspects, Angela told Conner the real story, and his reporting reopened the case. She taught Conner all the little details of police work that her macho colleagues tended to keep secret from their spouses—the frustrating drudgery of the job; the mind-numbing paperwork; her superiors' mendacity and bigotry, no matter their race or ethnicity.

What excited Conner about writing *Devil Shotgun* for Angela was that he knew she would give him her honest opinion and tell him everything that rang false. Her unvarnished speech, her refusal to say what he may have wanted to hear, forced him to bring out his true self, the honesty that just about all writers strive for.

But coming home from LaGuardia, as he drove his Porsche past East Stroudsburg and then took the Delaware Water Gap exit to his house, he realized writing could become almost as exciting as it had been back then. Now he could write with no audience to please other than himself—not even Dex. For, even if he wrote a novel that Dex hated, he would still have his first two payments for whatever he had written, and that would be more than enough to live on for a very long time. He tried to regard Dex less as a potential nemesis and more as a benefactor, a modern Lorenzo de' Medici, his court populated with writers.

The moment he pulled into his driveway and saw Angela nursing Atticus on the front porch, he sensed he had made the right decision. Angela had stuck a For Sale by Owner sign into the front lawn, but Conner pulled it out and ripped it in half. And when Angela embraced him and then walked with him into the house and into the bedroom, where they made love while Atticus slept in his crib, he knew he was right. His only regret was that, for the first time since he'd met her, he would have to lie to her.

But lying to Angie, the one thing she had told Conner she would never be able to forgive, proved surprisingly easy. He told her he was working on a screen adaptation of one of his novels for a Hollywood production company, and she, having no interest in movies after *Devil Shotgun* had been butchered, didn't ask any more questions about what Conner was writing or how it had suddenly become so lucrative.

Conner and Angie tried to be smart about their money. They didn't buy another Porsche; in fact, they sold the Porsche and bought a Subaru Outback with plenty of room for multiple car seats, and started talking about having a second child. They put some of the money aside for Atticus's college fund and spent about ten grand to take care of the plumbing and leakage issues that were still bedeviling the house. They put fifty grand in their checking account and the rest in a money market account. They hadn't gone on a vacation since Atticus had been born, so they decided to take one, but they didn't go anywhere expensive. They rented an oceanfront cottage in a small lobstering community in northern Maine, where they spent their days walking along the slippery shores strewn with seaweed, black rocks, and mussel shells. They dipped their son's feet in the water and watched him toddle along the brown-black sand. In the evenings, after Angie put Atticus to sleep, Conner would take the manual typewriter and some paper and sit at a table by the ocean. He would listen to the cries of gulls and the fizzing ocean. He was full of ideas; words poured out of him.

"That sounds so perfect," I said to Conner as we sat on the bench above Griffy Lake.

"It really was," said Conner. "Or almost perfect. But there was at least one thing wrong with it."

"What was that?" I asked.

"I was writing the wrong thing," said Conner. "I had ideas for all kinds of books, but I couldn't think of a single idea for a thriller."

20

It only occurred to me later that I should have felt jealous of Conner and that it was presumptuous of him to burden me with his woes. After all, his troubles seemed far less vexing than mine—he had, at the very least, eight hundred grand to burn. Depending on which newspaper you read, a double-dip recession was either already in progress or on its way; the stock market was doing OK, but Sabine and I had invested our money in a politically correct, socially conscious fund managed by Indiana Mennonites, and all those investments had gone down the crapper. My retirement account, meager as it was, had been cut in half. I had been out of the workforce since our move to Indiana and lacked the appropriate skills and HTML coding and digital audio editing experience and whatever the hell else to jump back into journalism; the colleges and universities where Sabine was applying to teach were offering buyouts and instituting hiring freezes; my wife and I stood to lose not only her job and our comparatively easy lifestyle but also our health care and benefits. Even one-twentieth of the money Dex Dunford had already paid Conner would have allayed some of our fears and bought us breathing room.

But there on the bluff overlooking Griffy Lake, where all I could see was a calm, rippling lake, two small fishing boats upon it, and where no Dex Dunford or any Eastern European henchman was in sight, all I wanted was to listen to my friend tell a story. I just hoped I could prove as helpful to him as he seemed to think I could be. I half hoped he had tracked me down because he wanted me to tackle the writing assignment that had given him so much trouble in Maine. Maybe I could be the one to write the detailed, expertly researched thriller. I felt certain I could do it if the price were right.

"Maybe you need some help," I said. "A writing partner? Or an outside editor? Someone to bounce ideas off of?"

Conner smiled. "Thanks, man," he said. "But it's a little late for that. I already wrote the son of a bitch, but it's not exactly what I thought I was gonna write."

"You wrote a thriller?" I asked.

"Yeah, kinda," he said with sad resignation. A light rain was beginning to fall from the charcoal-colored clouds. "But you shoulda seen me before I started really writing it, man. For those few weeks, I was on fire. I was writing every sort of story you can imagine. I was writing a love story, I was writing a kids' book. I wanted to write a book for Angie; I wanted to write one for Atticus; hell, man, I was even thinking of writing a book about friendships and fathers and sons. It even crossed my mind that I should dedicate it to you. For real."

"That's not what Dex wanted you to write, though," I said.

"Uh-uh. He wanted a thriller, and that's the only book I didn't feel like writing anymore."

"Did you give up?"

"I thought about it for a while. I figured the hell with it. I tried to call you to get your take, but you weren't around. So I just went with my gut. I told myself I would write the book I wanted to write, see where it led. Maybe I could turn it into a thriller somehow."

But he couldn't. His mood was too light and thrillers were too dark. He spent a month with Angie and Atticus in Maine, getting more and more frustrated, and during that time, it occurred to him that maybe he could return the money to Dex. Maybe he could say he just didn't have any ideas for thrillers anymore and then he could take all his new ideas and use them to sell his next book to Shascha. Maybe she would like to see a romantic novel or one that he would write for his son.

Conner put the thriller out of his mind and made an appointment to meet with Shascha. "The only thing I wanted was to give Shascha a really good story, the best I'd ever written," said Conner. "Never in a million years did I think she would give me the idea for a story about a perfect crime."

21

I had never met Shajilah Shascha Schapiro, but I knew her reputation. Legendarily solicitous of her authors, she was equally standoffish when it came to showing herself in public. She didn't do the New York publishing party scene, didn't chat up journalists or would-be novelists. When I worked at *Lit* and called her office asking for a quote or two to fill out my article about Conner, she didn't return my calls. She had her assistant, Courtney Guggenheim, dictate a two-sentence response so boring, noncommittal, and generic that I didn't wind up using it, which was probably Shascha's intention. The only publication she was ever quoted in was the *New York Times*.

Shascha possessed everything you might expect a New York editor with her very own imprint at a major publishing house to possess. Her background spoke to both material and cultural wealth—her father was a hotshot in international finance; her mother a flautist with the New York Philharmonic. Her parents were on the board of just about every cultural institution and charitable foundation in the city. Shascha herself had an intimidating résumé—the Chapin School, graduated from Harvard in three years, aced the Radcliffe Publishing Program, youngest junior editor ever at Schreiber & Sons, fastest to acquire her own imprint.

Few people would dispute her beauty, but in the handful of pictures she permitted anyone to publish, she was almost more of a representation of beauty than a beautiful woman in her own right. With her long straight black hair, her sparkling green eyes, her golden skin, her commanding stature—even in flats, she stood six feet tall—she was powerful, intimidating, and statuesque in the truest sense of the word. She looked as though she had been sculpted, not born.

But what made Shascha exceptional, aside from her striking presence, exquisite taste, and sharp editorial instincts—qualities many in her profession possessed—was her ability to envision books and authors in their entirety, to know not only whether a book was good or marketable but also how it would perform over the years, how its author would be perceived, how authors and books could be packaged. She was as much soothsayer as editor. Fifteen different publishing houses had passed on *The Unmitigated Empty*, the first installment of Margot Hetley's Wizard Vampire Chronicles series, but not only did Shascha pay $3 million for that book and its first two sequels, she reenvisioned Hetley—a foulmouthed former heroin addict, petty criminal, and rock 'n' roll groupie who had done time for larceny and had only one memoir to her credit—as a tart-tongued role model for teenagers who would go over big time on *Oprah*, *Ellen*, and *The View*. When Shascha's stylists were done with her, Margot's saucy good looks came to suggest the actress Helen

Mirren in her prime; her unpolished Yorkshire accent gave her the everywoman approachability of the singer Susan Boyle. What Shascha perceived, Margot Hetley became to tens of millions of readers.

When Shascha purchased *Devil Shotgun*, she envisioned an entire series of thrillers. With subdued cityscape cover images and somber, black-and-white author photos, she positioned Conner as a thinking man's genre novelist whose books could stand alongside those of Michael Connelly and Dennis Lehane. That bet had not paid off as well as Shascha had hoped, but most of her bets did.

As for her personal life, Shascha kept it well hidden. In the *New York Times* Style section, she had been linked romantically with everyone from conductor Gustavo Dudamel to the actor Paul Giamatti to Condoleezza Rice. Rumors ran the gamut: she was a raging nymphomaniac; a transsexual; a virgin saving herself for marriage—as far as anyone knew, she was still single. Over the years, Shascha had been loyal to Conner, a good deal more loyal than she tended to be with authors whose spotty sales record matched his. Perhaps, some speculated, she was secretly hoping for an affair with Conner—after all, he was one of the only male authors in her stable.

On the day of his meeting with Shascha, Conner drove his Subaru to Scranton, Pennsylvania, and took the bus into the city. On the ride over in the quiet car, he considered the conversation he and Shascha would have. He wanted to change directions, he would say. He had more in him than Cole Padgett novels.

The Schreiber & Sons Building on Seventh Avenue had something in common with Shascha Schapiro herself—tall, commanding, elegant, and more than a little cold. It was forty stories of steel and glass with a lobby that Leni Riefenstahl might well have filmed had she been making movies about publishers instead of Olympic athletes and Nazis. Schreiber had published some of the greats, many of whose works could be found in the three-story, glass-enclosed shelves in the lobby, and in the windows that gave out onto Seventh Avenue, where authors such as Margot Hetley were represented.

Conner felt confident as he strode toward the revolving front doors, but when he noticed a pair of police cars and a black limousine with tinted windows stalled out front, he became wary. There was a pair of navy-blue-suited men who were speaking into mouthpieces. They eyed Conner as he approached the revolving doors. "How're you doin', fellas?" Conner asked, but neither responded. Strange, Conner thought, but then again, Schreiber & Sons published the works of many world leaders, so perhaps Bill Clinton or Henry Kissinger was on the premises, meeting about a memoir.

Conner walked straight past two police officers milling about in the Schreiber lobby, and headed for the front desk, where longtime security chief Steve Kaczmarak was stationed.

"How's it goin', Steve?" asked Conner, but the uncharacteristically humorless, uniformed man at the front desk looked blankly at Conner.

"ID, please, sir," Steve said.

"ID?" asked Conner. "You know me, man. I've been coming here for seven years."

"They told me to check everybody's ID, no matter who it is, sir."

Conner laughed. "What's going on? Is the president in town?"

"I'm sorry, I can't tell you that, Mr. Joyce."

Conner was about to ask why Steve was calling him "Mr. Joyce," but he let the matter go. He waited for Steve to call Courtney Guggenheim to confirm his appointment. Then Steve issued Conner an ID and directed him to the elevators.

Though his first journeys to Shascha's office during the early days of *Devil Shotgun* had always filled Conner with a sense of accomplishment, importance, and potential, that feeling had waned with each subsequent book until he had begun to feel like an uninvited guest, or if not uninvited, then invited only out of courtesy. But now, as he stepped out of the elevator and onto Shascha's floor, that sense of possibility was returning. He had more than eight hundred grand in savings and so didn't truly need Shascha to publish the books he had come to discuss.

Courtney Guggenheim met Conner at the glass doors. Whether Courtney was actually an heiress to the Guggenheim fortune was something no one at the publishing house had been able to find out for sure, but the surname, in addition to her looks, her fierce ambition, and her Ivy League pedigree, had gotten her the gig, and in a few years' time would most probably get her an even better one.

Courtney greeted Conner with a hug and a cheek kiss. She was wearing a magenta dress, a pink rose in her hair, and matching high heels with which she walked across the gray carpet as effortlessly as if she were wearing sneakers.

"So, what's with all the security downstairs?" Conner asked Courtney as he tried to keep up with her.

Courtney grinned. Her expression was that of a woman who had been sworn to secrecy and loved the sense of authority her prized knowledge gave her.

"Shascha's around today, isn't she?" Conner asked. They were walking quickly past cubicles in which editorial assistants were slaving over manuscripts on desktop computers. In offices with closed doors, grim-faced senior editors, red pencils in their mouths or poised in one hand, punctiliously sliced up manuscripts.

"She's meeting with somebody," said Courtney.

"Who with?"

Usually, Courtney loved being pressed for information, grudgingly surrendering it as if she had no other choice. This time, her smile broadened but she offered nothing more than a knowing little melody—*"Dee-dah-dee-dah-dee,"* she sang.

The door to Shascha's office was closed, so Conner stopped at Courtney's cubicle. Manuscripts flagged with yellow stickies with "Out" written on them were stacked and rubber-banded. Letters from agents were filed in color-coded folders. Even Courtney's computer screen was exquisitely organized—folders were arranged in alphabetized rows. But what caught Conner's eye and forced him to linger was a stack of signed eight-by-ten photos of Margot Hetley with her wavy blond hair and big black eyes.

"Is that who Shascha's meeting with?" Conner asked.

"Dee-da-dee-da-dee," said Courtney.

"Is she delivering her new manuscript or something?"

"Doo-dah-doo-dah-doo."

Just about every major publishing house had a franchise superstar author such as Margot Alexandra Hetley in its catalog. Franchise authors' book sales paid the salaries of the Courtney Guggenheims of the world, and underwrote the advances for Conner Joyce novels, as well as *Nine Fathers*, now that I think of it. At Doubleday, Dan Brown was the franchise; at Little, Brown, it was James Patterson. At Merrill Publishers, it was Blade Markham. When these authors made their deadlines, editors got year-end bonuses; when they didn't and the annual profit-and-loss statements didn't add up, entire departments got axed. Younger editors with more uncompromising literary tastes and more idealistic mind-sets than their superiors would grumble in secret or in pseudonymous Twitter posts about the franchise authors' lousy writing. They would criticize their bosses for selling out, make fun of the franchise authors' grammar and spelling. But Shascha Schapiro and her ilk knew better; without a few Margot Hetleys, publishing could not survive, and these authors were afforded every perk imaginable. Three-course lunches, executive suites, personal drivers, and business-class travel were just the beginning; even lapses in common decency were immediately forgiven, if they were noticed at all.

Which was why, when the door to Shascha Schapiro's office opened and Margot Hetley, in the flesh, asked Conner Joyce, "What the fuck're you starin' at, mate?" then cupped her breasts, waggled them mockingly, and asked, "Ain't you never seen a pair?" no one thought to admonish her or to apologize to Conner, who had been planning only to say hello to Margot and to tell her how much his wife enjoyed her work. Courtney clapped her hands together and giggled as if Ms. Hetley had told a splendid joke. And Shascha gave Margot a warm embrace, telling her how good it had been to see her again, and to have a pleasant flight back to London. Margot told Shascha, "Take good care of my baby," then added, "you certainly paid a lot for the little bugger." No one introduced Conner to Margot; he tried to win her over with a smile.

"My wife loves your books," he essayed.

"Tell the cunt to get in line," Hetley said, then gave a nod to the men on her security detail. She strutted down the hallway with Courtney Guggenheim guiding her out.

Conner followed Shascha into her office; Shascha shut the door.

22

The light drizzle falling on the Overlook Trail had resolved itself into an insistent rain, and even though Conner and I were partially protected by the branches of tulip trees, our clothes were getting wet and Hal, not exactly a fan of damp weather, was growling and pulling me back toward the path. The way down was treacherous, and by the time we made it back to our cars, my sneakers and pants were dirty from the few spills I had taken. Hal was wet too, his tail muddy; he looked pissed.

I asked Conner if he wanted to continue our conversation in a café, but he said no, he didn't want to go anywhere people might overhear us. And though he thanked me for suggesting that we go back to my house, he said he didn't want to bother my family. So we sat in my Volvo, watching the rain petal the windshield and our view of Lake Griffy. The car was stuffy and smelled like wet dog and

Conner's cologne, but every time I cracked a window, my sleeve got wet and Hal whined, so I shut the window and tried not to feel claustrophobic.

"How did your meeting with Shascha go?" I asked.

"About as well as I probably should have expected," said Conner.

"What does that mean?"

"I think you can figure that out."

"Yeah. I guess I can."

For an editor as accomplished and haughty as Shascha, one might have expected her to work in a corner office with a breathtaking view of the Hudson. Her office was, in fact, in a corner; whether or not the view was good was difficult to say. She kept all her blinds drawn and relied on the overhead fluorescents and her desk lamps for illumination. Her desk, unlike those of her senior editors and her assistants, was spotless, unsullied by manuscripts or correspondence. Save for her telephone, desktop computer, and keyboard, there was nothing on it except a framed picture of herself shaking hands with the president at a White House dinner, a photograph of her parents' wedding, and a small robin's-egg-blue Tiffany jewelry box, inside which was what looked like a monogrammed flash drive encrusted with tiny diamonds. With other editors, the barren desk might have been a sign of laziness, of the traditional image of the high-power publisher who delegates all work to underpaid assistants so that she can spend her time planning vacations and lunches and bemoaning her arduous work schedule and the state of contemporary publishing in a postliterate age. But with Shascha, it was a sign of her discretion; when an author was in her office, he or she was never reminded of the fact that Shascha worked with other authors. If she was meeting with you, it was as if she were your only reader. Dex Dunford wasn't the only person who could make writers feel that way.

As he sat across from Shascha, Conner spoke eloquently and at length about his frustration with his Cole Padgett books. He was excited about taking his writing in a new direction. He summarized a few of the stories he had been developing, hoping to inspire the energetic back-and-forth exchanges he'd had with Shascha in the past. But as he proceeded, he became painfully conscious of the fact that Shascha wasn't interrupting him as she usually did; she was letting him say whatever he wanted while she checked e-mail on her iPhone and scrolled through book sales for her other authors on Bookscan. She answered messages, read the headlines of the *New York Times* and *Publishers Lunch*. Conner began to feel as though he were a convicted criminal, allowed to speak to the judge and jury after they had already completed his sentencing.

"So," Conner said as he wrapped up his monologue, "that's what I'm thinking of doing—branching out. But I'm not sure whether I should start by writing that kids' book or the more romantic novel, or whether you think I should still be trying to write another Cole Padgett book. If you think that's the way to go, I could give it another shot." He let his voice drift off, waiting for Shascha to respond. She had always been good about giving straight, authoritative advice, telling Conner exactly what he needed to do in order to, say, make his characters more sympathetic or to add a bit of romance for his female readers.

Today, she said only this: "Well, I'm sure whomever you wind up publishing with will have a better idea of what the market is like at that time, and you should probably rely on their opinion."

Doom was sealed inside Shajilah Schapiro's words, but Conner wasn't certain he had heard it. "Whomever I wind up publishing with?" he asked.

Shascha smiled grimly and eyed Conner with a wistful gaze that suggested disappointment with what could have happened, but never did, and now never would.

"Fewer books, bigger books, that's our new mantra over here," Shascha said. "If we don't think a book will sell a hundred thousand copies right off the bat, we can't afford to be interested in it. You're a talented guy, and you've done well for yourself and we've done well for you, but right now, our margins are too tight."

"So, if I'm not Margot Hetley . . ." Conner began.

"It's brutal," said Shascha, "but that's where the business is right now." She sat up straight in her chair, while Conner remained slumped in his. His attention was now riveted to the only unusual item on Shascha's otherwise uncluttered desk—the bejeweled flash drive nestled in white tissue paper in the Tiffany box. He stared at that flash drive, and as he did, he became conscious that it was monogrammed with gold letters—MAH. Margot Alexandra Hetley.

Take care of my baby; you certainly paid a lot for the little bugger, Hetley had told Shascha before she left. The next installment of Wizard Vampire Chronicles—WVCIX—was right there. A priceless book encapsulated on a device as small as a skipping stone.

"What is that?" Conner asked.

Shascha didn't answer.

"Is that what I think it is?" he asked.

Shascha closed the box, placed it in a desk drawer, closed that drawer firmly, locked it, then stood up and walked Conner to the front door.

"I'm sorry, Conner, but I really do have to cut this short," Shascha told him. "I have a lunch." She said he should call her the next time he was in the neighborhood and that he should give her regards to Angela. She asked if Conner wanted any books to take with him, but Conner said no, he didn't want any books. And so she grazed his cheek with a dry kiss, then shut her office door firmly behind him.

As Conner walked down the hallway, slowly yet inexorably, toward the exit, he studied the surroundings, knowing this would probably be the last time he would see them. He focused on small details. The whole place suddenly struck him as antiseptic, corporate, so far removed from his idealized image of literature in the heyday of J. D. Salinger and Harper Lee. He had never realized how white the walls were, how silent the offices. All he could hear was an electronic hum and the light clicking of fingers typing upon keyboards. No one stood to greet him, no one walked him to the door; Courtney Guggenheim was focusing on a manuscript on her tablet. For a moment, he thought he had become invisible, that Shascha Books had disappeared him. He could imagine himself in a scene in a James Bond film—"You don't exist, Mr. Bond. You never did. Your identity has been wiped clean." He had no editor anymore, no publisher; he still had an agent, but what could she tell him? The only prospect he had left was the book he was supposed to write for Dex Dunford, the one he hadn't been able to start because he had so many newer, supposedly better ideas. He had thought he was done with thrillers. But when he stepped out of the elevator and walked through the lobby of Schreiber & Sons, where Margot Hetley's security detail had already left, and security chief Steve Kaczmarak was greeting Conner by his first name again, he began to think he might have an idea for a thriller after all.

"I knew exactly what I was gonna do. I was gonna write another heist book," Conner told me as we sat in the car.

"About a flash drive, perchance?" I asked.

"You got it, buddy," said Conner. "A valuable goddamn bejeweled flash drive."

23

The rain had let up, but Conner said he still didn't really want to go anywhere, so we wound up driving around the back roads of Bloomington, passing this and that nature preserve, passing the chain stores and fast-food restaurants along the bypass, driving around the university campus, through the quiet, homey neighborhoods where I used to think my children would grow up. I had never particularly cared for this place, but now I viewed it with a sensation approaching nostalgia. It was a place comfortably free of ambition or expectation. Maybe Conner had been right to seek me out here—even if someone had overheard us, no one would have believed this discussion of big book contracts, unpublished Salinger manuscripts, nefarious skullduggery, and cockeyed flumdummery would happen here.

"But exactly how would someone steal the flash drive?" I asked Conner.

"So easily," he said. "So, so easily, my friend. Or at least it could be if you were writing a novel about it."

Throughout the history of literature, every publishing company has had special protocols for dealing with its most important manuscripts. In the old days of tweed and cigars, of manual typewriters and carbon paper, critics or journalists who wanted an early look at an important forthcoming novel by, say, Ernest Hemingway or J. D. Salinger, would sit with a copy of the page proofs in the publisher's office, reading while an editorial assistant kept watch, making sure the journalist didn't steal it. In some cases, journalists were not even allowed to take notes, or if they did, they had to share those notes with an editor before they departed.

At *Lit* magazine, I got a chance to visit the J. R. Kenworth printing plant in Lancaster, Pennsylvania, where I interviewed the longtime plant foreman Mitch McGauhey about some of the books that had been printed there. Sometimes, he told me, special measures had to be taken when a particularly controversial book was being printed—say, something like *Lolita* or *Portnoy's Complaint*, both of which had led workers to walk off the job rather than participate in the production of something they felt was pornographic. Therefore, manuscripts of this sort would arrive at the plant with dummy covers and fake title pages, identifying them as academic books or yawn-worthy biographies of American presidents. Some editions of *The Satanic Verses* had been printed in that plant, but because of the bomb threats issued against anyone associated with the production or publication of Salman Rushdie's novel, no one in the plant knew they were printing it. In the case of J. K. Rowling's Harry Potter series, the title given to the third book, *Harry Potter and the Prisoner of Azkaban*, was *Manuscript #110*. It was printed on July 4, 1999, when the plant was supposedly closed for Independence Day and the only people allowed in had undergone rigorous security checks.

These days, with rampant digital piracy and hundreds of free P2P file-sharing sites, when one could download the digital file of a manuscript in seconds with a mere click of a mouse, the stakes were greater, and so were the risks. Most probably, that explained the security forces accompanying Margot Hetley. That certainly explained the Tiffany jewel box with the diamond-encrusted, monogrammed flash drive that Shascha kept in her locked drawer.

More than anyone else, save, perhaps, for Margot Hetley herself, Shascha understood how much the ninth installment of Wizard Vampire Chronicles was worth. In short, it was just the sort of item whose theft would make for a good, original heist thriller. The list of suspects seemed endless, and those suspects weren't the sort who usually appeared in genre thrillers—editors, authors, security personnel. Anyone who worked in the Schreiber & Sons Building, any of Shascha's employees, would have had a strong motive for committing that sort of theft. If, in real life, someone found a way to break into Shascha's office and take that flash drive, everyone would have been under suspicion—Steve Kaczmarak, the supposedly loyal security guard; Courtney Guggenheim, who, like most editorial assistants, probably had dreams of writing her own books and no doubt was tired of taking orders from Shascha; even, and perhaps most likely, Conner Joyce, or someone like him, a recently terminated author who had been insulted by Hetley and needed to devise a new way to support his family.

Once someone got hold of that flash drive, the rest would be easy. The thief or thieves could set up a website, maybe one overseas, spread the word through Twitter and other social-networking sites that pirated copies of WVCIX were available. Then the thieves would take credit-card orders, assemble e-mail addresses, and click Send All. They would collect the money, then close down the site. How much money could you make? Two and a half million seemed conservative.

While writing his Cole Padgett books, Conner had always thought the best way to become a criminal would be to lead as honest a life as he and Angie had, then gamble everything on one crime. The more he thought about it, he almost wanted to commit this particular crime instead of writing about it. *Almost.* He would have considered it if he were a different sort of person. And when he wrote the book, the character based on him would be the thief, for he was the most plausible suspect of all.

Yes, Conner Joyce thought as he walked toward Penn Station to catch his train, there really could be a thriller in this.

24

Conner spent six hours a day writing in his home office in the Pokes, using the Smith-Corona manual typewriter that he had saved from his boyhood, making edits with J. D. Salinger's old Montblanc pen. He told Angie he was working on "that Hollywood project," and didn't want to discuss it for fear of jinxing it. She may have been suspicious, but she didn't ask any questions.

Work on the novel proceeded quickly. Conner knew the situation, the crime, and the potential suspects. He knew Dex wanted details, so he provided them. There was no danger of libeling anyone, since no one would ever read the novel save Dex and perhaps Pavel and the ghost of Truman Capote, so he used real names, places, and addresses. He usually conducted copious amounts of research for his novels, but since he knew the individuals involved, where they worked, and their personality quirks, there was little need. He knew what it was like to be a frustrated writer on the road, trying to maintain his enthusiasm in front of an audience of a dozen people in a shopping-mall chain store that was going out of business; he knew how it felt to argue with his wife when both were overwhelmed by parenthood and felt uncertain about their futures; he knew every inch of the lobby of Schreiber & Sons and Shascha's floor; he knew how it felt to wait outside Shascha's office while she met with Margot Alexandra Hetley; he knew how it might feel to lose everything, then catch sight of a small, priceless object that could save him and his family. He knew what could make an honest man turn to crime, the way it always happened in his novels.

The only trouble with the book was that it just wasn't all that sexy. His own life story, unlike those of his recluse writer heroes J. D. Salinger, Jarosław Dudek, B. Traven, Harper Lee, and their ilk didn't seem compelling enough for a thriller. There were no knives or guns, just a valuable document with a compromised password and a stolen flash drive. So he did something he had rarely done in his Cole Padgett novels; he embellished. The doggedly earnest, first-person narrator, with his faithful wife, adorable young son, and lovely home in the Poconos seemed too wholesome and dull, so he made the guy into a scumbag. He gave the narrator a handlebar mustache, tight jeans, flowery shirts open to the chest, a drawer full of gold medallions, and a sex addiction. The *Ice Locker* readings he had given in various bookstores throughout the country weren't dramatic, so his narrator seduced bookstore managers and autograph hounds, then took them back for wild sex in his author's suites, which were appointed far more lavishly than the ones in which he tended to stay.

He did much the same thing for the rest of the characters in the novel. He broadened all of their personalities and gave each of them even more credible motives for stealing the flash drive. The narrator's wife, Angie, became a nymphomaniac who had been thrown off the NYPD for coke abuse; Shascha Schapiro had actually bedded down with Condoleezza Rice and Gustavo Dudamel, and her publishing imprint was about to go bust while her father had been nailed for insider trading; Courtney Guggenheim was no Guggenheim after all—her real name was Corey Podmolik, a con artist from Greenpoint, Brooklyn, who had done time for kiting checks and was just waiting for the right occasion to take down her boss; Steve Kaczmarak, the Schreiber security chief, had a gambling problem and a juice loan to the mob that he had to pay off in thirty days. Put briefly, Conner made every guy in his novel a scheming stud, every woman a money-hungry skank; he embellished every single real-life character save for the one he didn't need to embellish: Margot Hetley, whose tart questions and insults ("Ain't you never seen a pair?" "Tell the cunt to get in line") he toned down considerably. Sometimes in fiction you had to mute reality in order to make it seem more believable.

Writing the book was as liberating as Dex said it would be. Knowing Angie would never read it—as stipulated by Dex, he locked the manuscript in his desk whenever he was finished for the day—allowed Conner to explore aspects of himself he would have otherwise kept private. He could indulge his wildest fantasies, live out each of his unlived lives without fear of repercussions, perhaps a little bit like a man imagining nine different fathers. Conner's narrator wasn't really him, but who he might have become had circumstances been different, had his parents divorced, say, or had he never known his dad. As he wrote, he silently thanked Dex for allowing him to write whatever he wanted without any fear of judgment. All writers should be so lucky, he thought; everyone should have the right to put whatever crazy thoughts he or she had on paper without wondering what critics or psychoanalysts would say or whether readers would buy it, or whether any family members would get pissed. He now understood why so many writers had agreed to Dex's proposal. It was as if he were being paid to dream, and who could say no to that?

Certainly not me, I thought as I drove around the Walnut Creek neighborhood of Bloomington, listening to Conner's story, looking at all the For Sale signs on houses I had once thought I might have a chance to buy. I would have done anything if I could have been paid to write my first novel as long as no one else read it. What wouldn't I have given to go back in time and make sure no one could read the blog Sabine and I wrote? It was too late for me, but not for Conner. At least, that's the way it seemed at the time.

25

The final manuscript clocked in at three hundred pages, the exact same length as *Devil Shotgun*, yet considerably shorter than any of its sequels, which had grown more convoluted with each installment. When Conner was finished typing, he shredded each of his previous drafts and burned his notes on his charcoal grill while he prepared salmon for dinner one evening. He read over the manuscript three times after he had finished it, fixed the spelling and grammar, and retyped it; each time he read the book, he liked it better. The characters were vivid, the dialogue crisp, the descriptions spare but effective. He felt alternately sorry that no one but Dex and Pavel would ever get to read it and relieved that no one would; he regretted that even he would never get a chance to read the novel again once he had given it to Dex, and that it would exist only in his memory and in a strange bookcase in Chicago beside other volumes only Dex and Pavel could read.

He gave his book a title—*The Embargoed Manuscript*—and then put it in a manila folder, placed that folder in his center desk drawer, locked it, and contemplated how he would get it to Dex. They had never discussed exactly how, when, and under what circumstances he would submit the finished manuscript. Dex had said only that he would be "in touch" and that he would not give Conner a deadline. But just a few days later, Conner stepped outside to pick up his newspaper and noticed a sealed, unstamped envelope sticking out of his mailbox. He opened the envelope and found a train ticket to Penn Station and a short note on Dex's stationery written in that distinctive, loopy handwriting—*Keens Steakhouse, tomorrow, 1PM, Dex.*

Keens. It almost seemed as if Dex were making a joke at his expense; this was the very steakhouse where Shascha had taken Conner to celebrate her purchase of *Devil Shotgun*. But at the same time, Keens, much like the Coq d'Or Lounge and the long-defunct Gold Star Sardine Bar, was Dex's sort of place too. It was a serious, old-style business executive's establishment—white tablecloths, dark-brown leather banquettes, blood-red steaks, professional waiters with Teutonic demeanors and occasionally Teutonic accents, well-fed diners in dark suits already on their third Dewar's by noon.

The next day, Conner arrived at Keens promptly at one, carrying his manuscript in a black leather satchel. Dex and Pavel were already drinking cocktails, and the grim-faced Deutsche maître d' led Conner to their table, where a bottle of Champagne was chilling in a pewter ice bucket. Dex stood, smiled, and shook Conner's hand; Pavel's expression, as always, seemed harder to pin down.

"I believe there may be cause for celebration," said Dex. Though Conner wondered how Dex knew this was true, he didn't ask.

After the men had ordered their steaks and Dex had directed the waiter to pop and pour the Champagne, Conner took the manuscript out of his satchel and handed it to Dex, who spent some time contemplating the title. Pavel spoke first.

"*The Embargoed Manuscript*," he said. "I like *thees* title very, very *motch*."

Dex flashed Pavel a look, then skimmed the first two pages. He sipped his Champagne, then placed the manuscript in an attaché case that had been leaning against one of the legs of his chair. He zipped that case closed.

"You work fast," said Dex.

"I was inspired," Conner said.

"By the story or the money?" asked Dex.

"Maybe both."

"As it should be," said Dex.

"But what happens if you lose it?" asked Conner.

"The money?" asked Dex.

"The manuscript."

"I'll never let it out of my sight, and Pavel never lets me out of his." Dex reached into his inner jacket pocket and produced a check made out to Conner for $833,333.33. On the memo line, Dex had written the words "Upon Submission."

"I'd still like to know where your money comes from," Conner said.

"The answer would only wind up disappointing you," said Dex.

"Because the truth wouldn't be as interesting as what I might imagine?"

"It never is," said Dex.

Conner folded the check and placed it in his wallet. He tried to act unimpressed. "I assume there'll be some revisions you'd like me to make to the manuscript?" he asked.

"I suppose there might be, yes," said Dex.

"And how will you let me know about those?"

"We'll assess that when it's necessary," said Dex.

"But how will I know whether or not you like what I've written?"

"When I pay you."

"So, you'll be reading the manuscript soon?"

"Relax, Conner," said Dex. "I am not a slow reader, but I do like to read at my own pace. I will finish when it is time for me to finish. Don't concern yourself with that. I have always paid my writers. And I have always done so after a reasonable number of revisions and within a reasonable time frame. That's really all you need to know."

At which point, Dex stopped discussing the details of the contract. Instead, he spoke of the Champagne lunches to which he had treated his other writers, the steak restaurants in various world capitals where he had entertained Truman Capote and John Updike.

"But what will happen to all the books they wrote?" Conner began, then stopped, feeling uneasy with where his thoughts had headed.

"You mean, after I die?" Dex asked.

"For example, yes," said Conner.

"They will be burned."

"Burned? Why?"

"Because that's the agreement," said Dex. "If something is intended to be private, it should remain so. Would you care for dessert?"

By now, Conner and I had driven along practically every major road in Bloomington. The end of the afternoon was approaching, rain was still falling lightly, and we were back in the parking lot of the Lake Griffy Nature Preserve; Conner's rented Nissan was the only car still there; the boats were gone; the boat sheds were padlocked.

"How long ago did you have that lunch with Dex and Pavel?" I asked.

"About three months ago," said Conner. "I suppose I don't need to tell you what happened next."

"Yeah," I said. "Actually, you do."

"You must not read the newspapers much," he said.

"Rarely get the chance these days." That was true. Lately, Sabine and I had been so preoccupied that whole weeks' worth of the *New York Times* and *Bloomington Times Herald* would lie on our front porch before we bothered picking them up, at which point we just chucked them in the recycling box. The only use we ever seemed to get out of the newspaper was for lining the compost bucket or entertaining Beatrice and Ramona with papier-mâché projects.

"Well," Conner began. He seemed to be settling in for the next chapter of his story, but when I checked the clock in the car, I knew I didn't have time to hear it. Not then, anyway. Soon, I would have to pick up the kids, and I hadn't even started dinner.

"Tonight, then," he said.

"It'll have to be late," I told him. In recent weeks, it had been taking even longer than usual to get our daughters to sleep, and I couldn't just walk out on Sabine without notice. She had papers to grade, lectures to prepare, recommendations and job letters to write. Besides, much as I felt somewhat starved for friendship, I couldn't help but feel that Conner was taking my availability for granted, as if I could easily change whatever I had scheduled to accommodate his story.

"I still don't get why you're telling me all this," I said.

"I think you already know," he said.

"If I knew, I wouldn't ask," I said.

"Well, how about this? You remember the line in that Le Carré book I told you about? 'Promise me that if ever I find the courage to think like a hero, you will act like a merely decent human being'?"

"Of course."

"Pretty soon, there may come a time when I'll have to act like a hero, and if that happens, I may have to ask you to act like a merely decent human being."

"What does that mean?" I asked. "What would I have to do? What are you trying to get me involved in?"

"I'm the one who's involved, not you," Conner said. "There's no risk for you. I'm the one taking the risk by coming here and talking to you."

"But what would I have to do?"

"Just tell my story. As honestly as you can," he said. "The way you told *Nine Fathers*."

"Couldn't you tell it yourself?"

"I'm not sure about that," he said. "Lately, I've been getting the feeling I might not be around long enough to tell it, and you're the only person I can trust with it. You get it, don't you?"

"Sure." But I didn't. Not really. For a long time, among my friends, I have had a reputation for being particularly honest and moral. It's a reputation I find flattering but inaccurate. I do listen fairly well, though, a talent people often mistake for trustworthiness. Because Conner was moral and honest, he saw those traits reflected in me, when in fact I was and still am a great deal less admirable than he thought. I wasn't listening to him because I sympathized or shared his opinions; I just liked a good story. I did feel flattered by his friendship, but even if I didn't, I wouldn't have known how to tell him no.

"Is that the only reason?" I asked. "Because you trust me?"

Conner considered for a moment. "Also because no one knows you," he said. "No one knows we're friends. And even if Dex did know, I'm sure he wouldn't wanna mess with you."

"With me?" I asked.

"That's right," said Conner.

"I think you've got the wrong guy," I said.

"No sir," said Conner. "Trust me."

26

I told Conner we could meet again after I'd told the kids their bedtime stories—*Lyle, Lyle, Crocodile* for Beatrice, a chapter of *All-of-a-Kind Family* for Ramona. I had grown to cherish those bedtime story hours more than any other part of the day. They marked the only times I could say unequivocally that I was doing something worthwhile. Watching my children's enchantment as I either read a story or made up my own, I understood that sometimes all a story needed was one or two people to read or listen to it to make it matter.

But as night fell, I grew leery. What did I really know about Conner other than what he had told me during our interviews? I remembered the first time Beatrice had seen his picture in the aisle of Borders, by now out of business and functioning on a month-to-month lease as Fireworks City. Beatrice had seemed frightened of him, and I wasn't willing to dismiss her instincts any more than I was willing to dismiss those of my generally easygoing dog, who had growled and barked when he had seen Conner approaching. What did Conner mean about deciding to be a hero and asking if I'd act like a decent human being in return by telling his story? Might he have been going mad? Might he have chosen me to listen not because Dex would never "mess with" me, whatever that was supposed to mean, or that he trusted me with his story, or that he wanted me to tell it in case something happened to him, but rather because deep down he knew I was the only one gullible enough to believe him?

We agreed to meet at the Starlite Drive-In Movie Theatre, a half hour out of town on Old State Route 37, midway between Bloomington and Indianapolis, where he would be catching his flight home. Driving north through Ku Klux Klan country in Martinsville with Miles Davis's "Elevator to the Gallows" playing loud on my Volvo's stereo, I worried I would attract attention being a single male attending the drive-in, and that when I got into Conner's car, or he got into mine, we would look like a couple of guys about to give each other hand jobs. But no one seemed to pay us any mind when I pulled into a space, Conner pulled his Nissan beside mine, and he got into the passenger seat of my car, patted me on the shoulder, and shook my hand.

"Hey buddy, what's the flick?" he asked.

"Dunno," I said. "I didn't even think to check. Let's take a look." But the credits were long since over; the movie was already more than halfway through. It was a cops-and-robbers movie—motorcycles, automatic weapons, and a strong hero who was a man of few words—the Rock or Vin Diesel or some other strapping dude I'd never seen in a movie before.

We began by discussing our usual topics—parenthood, literature, the lousy economy—and when we were done, Conner told the rest of his story. The violence on-screen seemed to underscore the elegant bloodlessness of Conner's tale of a purloined flash drive and an embargoed manuscript. But then again, as I had told Conner, I hadn't been reading the newspapers lately, and so I didn't know where Conner's story might be leading, and that it might not wind up being so different from the movie on-screen after all.

27

I expected to hear back from Dex in a few weeks, maybe a month at most," Conner said. His face flickered in the darkness, reflecting the images of the movie. The book he had written was quick and uncomplicated, the sort he imagined one could buy at an airport bookstore and finish during a New York–Chicago flight. For the first few weeks after giving Dex the manuscript, he wondered why he wasn't hearing back. He obsessed about the sorts of revisions Dex might request, the details he might want Conner to add. Maybe he wouldn't like the novel at all and would ask Conner to write something else.

Conner became haunted by the possibility he might never be done with the project, that Dex would keep pressing him to write and revise; conceivably, he could be working on the same story for decades. He would never publish a book again, would have to lie to Angie for the rest of his life, and all for the $1.66 million he had been paid so far, a great sum, to be sure, for the little work he'd done, but a less impressive number if spread across his lifetime. He wondered if that was why Salinger, Dudek, and Harper Lee ultimately stopped publishing; maybe they had spent the rest of their lives writing and rewriting for Dex. Nothing in the contracts he had seen would have prevented that from happening. Maybe none of them had been hiding from the public; maybe none of them really wanted to be recluses; maybe all of them had just been hiding from Dex.

Two months passed without a word from Dex or Pavel, and Conner began to think less about *The Embargoed Manuscript*. He busied himself with home-improvement projects—drywall, plumbing, repainting the nursery; he took Atticus for walks along the Delaware River; he wrote little stories for Atticus and for Angela, never wondering if he would ever publish them. He and Angela began having sex more frequently, trying for a second child. It would be lonely for Atticus in the Poconos, Angela said. She had grown up in a big family in Hamilton Heights; having a younger brother or sister would be good for the boy.

It was just about then, with life seeming more beautiful and filled with possibility than it had since the first days of his marriage, that Dex reappeared.

"He just showed up?" I asked.

"Well, it wasn't Dex exactly," said Conner. "I didn't see him, but he made his presence known. Are you sure you haven't read the papers?"

28

The Starlite Drive-In was showing a double feature, and the late show was a horror movie, something about a serial killer stalking high school kids. I had always been scared of horror movies. When I was a kid, my mom took me downtown with one of her boyfriends to see an old movie called *Laura* at the Carnegie Theatre. But before the movie began, there was a trailer for *The Last House on the Left*. It traumatized me. Truly. So much so that, when we watched *Laura*, I kept thinking that the movie's villain was my mom's boyfriend. And so, even though the audio was off at the drive-in and I wasn't watching the screen, every so often, some terrifying image would insinuate itself into my peripheral vision—a masked man wielding a knife; that same man plunging the knife into someone's flesh—and I couldn't help looking. Meanwhile, Conner didn't even seem to register the film on the screen; he was too involved in his own story.

"Hey, tell me something," he said. "Was it a nice day here the day before yesterday?"

"Not really," I said. "It's been raining all week."

"It was gorgeous in the Poconos, man," said Conner. "The first real warm day of spring. The sky was blue, not a cloud in it. I heard warblers, woodpeckers, nuthatches, all those gorgeous birds singin' all their gorgeous songs. It was as beautiful a day as it was on 9/11, you remember that day?"

"Yeah," I said, "I do." I had been working at *Lit,* and our office was only a mile and a half north of the World Trade Center. Later that day, even at my apartment all the way uptown, I could smell the smoke and the melting metal, and my dog hadn't been able to stop panting and whining. At the drive-in, I tried to rid myself of that memory. And I tried not to start at the screams coming from the other cars.

"Yeah," Conner said. "It was one of those days that was so beautiful, you almost knew it couldn't last."

It had been early morning; Conner had arisen before Angela and Atticus to take in the air and chop some firewood. Whenever he woke up early, the newspaper was already there waiting for him, but he rarely read it until later in the day. This time, for some reason, he decided to unwrap the paper. With his ax in one hand and the newspaper in the other, he sat down on the porch swing and unfolded the paper to read the front page. On it was a full-color image of a haggard Margot Hetley, shadows under her eyes; below her picture was a headline: DIGITAL PIRATES MAKE OFF WITH NEW WIZARD CHRONICLES; PUBLISHER AND AUTHOR STAND TO LOSE MILLIONS.

"Christ," Conner said to himself as he read the story. "He did it. The motherfucker went and did it."

As he sat on his porch swing, Conner looked up to see whether anyone was watching him; he saw no one—Atticus and Angela were inside; the nearest neighbor was half a mile away. But as he looked up, he noticed an envelope sticking out of his mailbox, even though it was far too early for the mail to have arrived and he was certain he had taken in the mail the day before.

Conner stood up; he dropped his ax to the ground. He turned the newspaper facedown on the porch swing. His face felt hot, his legs so unsteady he could barely make his way across the porch to his mailbox. He was afraid of what he might find, and yet he already knew what was inside.

III:
Upon
Acceptance

"One crime," Cole Padgett had taught him. "You're not a criminal if you commit just one crime. It's when you commit the second one— that's when what you are starts changing."

Conner Joyce, *Leap of Fate*

29

On the screen at the drive-in, the credits were rolling. Conner had taken his time telling me his story, and now the horror movie was over. All the other customers had driven their cars out of the Starlite parking lot. Only two cars remained—mine and Conner's.

"What was in the envelope?" I asked.

"I ripped it open," said Conner. "I expected there would be a letter inside, but there wasn't—just a check."

The check was made out to Conner for $833,333.33. On the memo line, Dex had written, "Upon Acceptance."

"Holy shit," I said.

"You said it, pal," said Conner. "But there was something else in there too."

"What?"

"A flash drive."

"Monogrammed?"

Conner took a long, deep breath. "Yes, my friend, it was."

As he stood on his porch in the Poconos, Conner held that flash drive in his hand and stared at it, wondering what exactly had happened and what he should do, when the door swung open and Angie appeared. She was holding Atticus in her arms. If Conner had been a more slippery character, one to whom lying came easily, he wouldn't have panicked. When Angie asked him what he had been looking at, he would have said something like, "Oh, nothing much." When she asked him what he was reading in the newspaper, he would have said, "Oh, just an article about my old editor; isn't that freaky?" When she saw him holding the flash drive and asked what it was, he would have said, "Just something I got from those rich folks in Hollywood." Then, he would have pocketed the flash drive, kissed Angie good morning, and asked her what she wanted for breakfast. He shouldn't have grabbed the newspaper and hidden the headline, then stormed into the house, demanding, "Why the hell can't I have at least a little peace in the morning?" He shouldn't have made a beeline for the upstairs bathroom and caused a big racket while flushing the damn flash drive down the toilet.

In fact, as he looked back on it, he had done just about everything wrong. He had overreacted to the flash drive and to the note from Dex. He had panicked when he saw the article in the newspaper, and, when Angie asked, "What the hell's the matter with you, CJ?" he tried too hard to act as though everything were normal. He explained way too much. He said he had eaten "something weird" at dinner and that's why he had run to the john. And, after he had made a plane reservation to Chicago, a fairly odd thing to do if he was, as he claimed, going to meet with "those Hollywood guys," he talked more than ever about the "writing project" and how "demanding" the aforementioned Hollywood guys were.

Maybe he should have just stayed put, maybe he should have just read the article in the paper, destroyed the flash drive, cashed the check, and moved on with his life. Dex and Pavel had obviously used his novel to steal the flash drive, but nothing connected Conner to the crime. When John Lennon was murdered, a copy of *Catcher in the Rye* was in Mark David Chapman's pocket, yet no one ever accused J. D. Salinger of being his accomplice. All Conner had thought he was doing was writing a story, getting every detail right, the same thing he had done with every one of his books. He wondered if this had always been Dex's intention or if Dex had just read his book and had seen an opportunity. He felt responsible for the theft, and at the same time, he felt a bit awed by his own mind. He had read stories about people who turned their dreams into reality; it was a recurring theme in Jarosław Dudek's novel, poems, and memoirs. Had Dex used all of his writers for this purpose? Had he commissioned crime novels from every writer he met, then committed those crimes, or had Conner been the first one, just lucky enough to write the crime that Dex could actually commit? He had to see Dex again, not only to discover the answers to these questions but to answer the new questions he had about himself. Was this who he truly was? Was there all that much difference between conceiving a crime and committing it? Was he good at this?

Once he had decided to go to Chicago, Conner didn't even pack a bag. He just bought a plane ticket and drove to LaGuardia on Angie's old motorcycle, the one with the Devil Shotgun exhaust pipes. He figured he would go straight to 680 N. Lake Shore Drive, buzz Dex's apartment, and if Dex wasn't there he'd leave a message and go to the Coq d'Or Lounge. But after he boarded the plane and fastened his seat belt, he noticed a broad-shouldered man in a tweed jacket and wrinkled black slacks hulking his way down the aisle, then taking the seat beside him. The man carried a black leather dopp kit and reeked of aftershave.

"Dex?" I asked.

"Pavel," said Conner.

Pavel sat down beside him, and Conner let loose with a flurry of whispered expletives. What had happened? What the fuck was going on?

"I suggest that you take these matters up with Dex," Pavel said.

"Where is he?" Conner felt fully prepared to whip off his seat belt, climb over Pavel, and have it out with Dex in first class, which was where he assumed Dex would be sitting. But Dex wasn't on their plane.

"He will meet us at airport," said Pavel. He added that he noticed Conner had not *pekked* a *begg*. He proffered his dopp kit to Conner. Dex had made a reservation for Conner at the Drake Hotel, he said.

"I'm not staying," said Conner. "After I get some things straight with Dex, I'm going home."

"This, of course, is up to you," said Pavel. He added that he had quite enjoyed *The Embargoed Manuscript* and thought it was Conner's strongest work since *Devil Shotgun*. He could tell that writing it had indeed been *"leeberating"* for Conner.

"What the hell are you? Some kind of book critic?" Conner was about to start swearing again. But then he felt himself torn between outrage and curiosity. "Wait, you read it?" he asked.

Pavel nodded.

"The whole thing?"

"That I did."

"You've read all of them, haven't you?"

"That I have."

Yes, Pavel said, he had read the Dudek, the Lee, the Hetley, the Mailer, the Capote, and the Pynchon. Yes, he had read them all.

"You read the Salinger."

"I did, yes."

"What was it about?"

"These matters, I must keep them confidential," Pavel said. "It's in the contracts, you understand." And then Pavel pointed out that the flight attendants were beginning to perform their safety demonstrations. Once those demonstrations were over, Pavel closed his eyes and slept through the entire flight.

"Of course, I didn't sleep at all," said Conner. Instead, he sat staring out the window, watching the lights of the city give way to blackness, then thick gray clouds, which persisted all the way to Chicago so that, for the majority of the flight, all he was able to see was his own reflection. Who was he? Who was he becoming? He was a rich man now by most estimates, and could become even richer the moment he deposited that final check from Dex. And yet, in doing so, he would be admitting his complicity, wouldn't he? Wasn't that why Dex had sent him the flash drive? To explain the costs of the money he had earned and the risks he would incur if he ever spoke of it to anyone? And yet, if you thought about it, he considered as he looked around at the other passengers on the airplane, wasn't every person here an accomplice to some sort of crime? Didn't everyone here pay taxes that supported all sorts of misbegotten military adventures? Wasn't supporting the airlines supporting their manufacturers, who probably built horrifying weapons systems as well? Living in a prosperous society in the twenty-first century, weren't we all complicit in something? Weren't we committing a crime every time we ate at McDonald's or filled up at a BP station or bought a pair of Nikes? And wasn't the crime Conner had aided and abetted a bloodless one that targeted only a couple of wealthy individuals? Sure, the logic might have been tortured, but wasn't there some truth to it? Wasn't everyone on this plane, in some way, guilty of something? Weren't they all working for Dex?

"This was yesterday?" I asked Conner.

"It was," he said.

A white pickup truck was driving around the parking lot of the Starlite Drive-In. It flashed its headlights twice before it pulled up alongside us. A rent-a-cop, probably in his sixties, wearing a state trooper's hat, lowered his window and motioned for me to do the same.

"Closing up here," he said. "Pretty soon we'll have to lock up the gates."

"We're just finishing up a conversation, bud," said Conner. "How long before you close?"

"Maybe fifteen minutes? Half hour?"

"Can we stay here till then?" asked Conner.

The cop shrugged, then drove off, steering his way through the lot as Conner continued his tale.

30

After Pavel and Conner passed through the terminal, they found Dex waiting for them on a bench at the O'Hare blue line elevated train station. He was dressed as usual, stylish but out-of-date, and he was carrying his walking stick with the yellow-eyed falcon handle.

"Public transportation? How come no limo? I'm sure you could afford one now," said Conner. He had wearied of the old-fashioned rituals of politesse that seemed to accompany all his interactions with Dex, all the "Good to see you, sir" and "Come, come, Mr. Joyce."

"Well, then I'd have to find a limo driver I could trust, and trust takes time," said Dex. "Anonymity is safer."

"Dex is very *parteeckular* about his employees," Pavel added. "For the right price, any one of them will betray you."

"Why not you?" Conner asked Pavel. "How come he trusts you

149

so much? What's he got on you? Immigration status problem? Or don't you speak good enough English to get by without his help?"

"It is because he has given me everything I have wanted, Mr. Joyce," Pavel said. "Just as he has given you everything you have wanted."

"What did he give you?" Conner asked.

"What we all want," said Pavel. "The opportunity to be free."

"You don't seem free to me," Conner said.

The train arrived. Its doors slid open and Conner followed the men into a mostly empty car. Conner sat in a window seat, Dex sat next to him, and Pavel on the bench behind as the train moved forward, accelerating out of the tunnel, following the eastward path of Interstate 90 toward the shimmering lights of downtown Chicago. Conner had seen those lights only once before, but this time they looked sinister; he felt drawn into the darkness that surrounded them.

"You seem different than when we last met," said Dex.

"How do you mean?" Conner asked.

"You appear upset."

"Of course I'm upset," said Conner.

"But why?" asked Dex. "Because I asked you to write a book and it gave me an idea? Isn't that why all writers write? To inspire their readers?"

"Not funny," said Conner.

"I'm not joking," Dex said.

"I'm not either. You straight-up lied to me."

"Me? Never. I despise liars. I hate them every bit as much as you do, Conner, and every bit as much as your wife does too."

"What's that supposed to mean?" asked Conner.

"You know exactly what it means," said Dex. "Don't play stupid; it's just another form of lying. You know I never actually lied to you."

"Then you misled me," said Conner.

"Only as much as you let yourself be misled," said Dex. "Only as much as Salinger, Dudek, Pynchon, Capote, and all the rest."

"Oh, bullshit," said Conner. "You did the same thing with all of them?"

"When their stories worked the way I wanted them to, absolutely, sir, I did."

"And how often did that happen?"

"Most of the time."

"And none of them objected when they found out?"

"Perhaps two or three did."

"And the others?"

"If they objected, they certainly didn't bother me about it."

"Salinger too?"

"He had some objections. Yes."

"And?"

"And he requested a few minor emendations to the contract."

"Did you agree to them?"

"Of course I agreed. He was my favorite, after all, still is my favorite, even now. But you know all this. I showed you the contracts. You read them."

"And then what did he say after you agreed?"

"All that he needed to."

"Which was what?"

"All that anybody needed to."

"And what was that?"

"He signed the contract and he deposited his check."

"Dudek too?" Conner asked.

"I have copies of each canceled check," said Dex. "I will not let you read the books they wrote; but I have shown you the contracts and I can show you the checks if you'd like."

"You don't have the last of mine," said Conner.

"Not yet, no," said Dex.

"I could just tear it up," said Conner.

"What possible good would that do?" asked Dex. "Donate it to charity. Support another writer. Feed someone's family. Don't merely *tear it up*. That's foolishness."

Conner was about to say something about integrity, but it seemed a little late for that. "So," he said, "you're telling me that of all the people who wrote books for you, I'm the first one who really raised any serious objection. Everyone honored their contracts, kept their mouths shut."

"If you were listening, you would know that I did not actually tell you that, sir," said Dex. "A couple raised a fuss. Some requested changes. Salinger added a rider, as you have already seen. One author even violated her contract outright."

"Who was that?" asked Conner.

"Lady Margot Hetley, in fact," said Dex, and when Conner asked for further explanation, Dex said, "She signed her contract. She wrote her book. She deposited her checks. And then she turned around, rewrote that same book, sold it, published it, then sold more than half a dozen others. You know the rest of that story."

"Doesn't seem to have hurt her career much, now has it?" said Conner.

"Not yet."

"What does that mean?"

"Why do you think she keeps those bodyguards, Conner? Because she's such a 'popular writer'?" Dex sighed. "Anyway, that's not the point I'm making. The point is after everything was said and done, all the writers cashed their checks. And my sense is that when they learned what had happened, they all grew to like the idea, just as you will grow to like the idea so much that you might even want to do it again."

"No way," said Conner.

"It doesn't satisfy you in the slightest?" asked Dex.

"What?"

"To know it worked? Your idea. To know you could write something that could become more than fiction?"

"But it didn't. You changed it. In the book, I steal the flash drive," said Conner. "It's the character based on me who does it."

"A small detail," said Dex.

"Who did it for real?" asked Conner.

Dex gestured to Pavel, who offered a self-effacing smile.

"You? How'd you even get into Shascha's office?" Conner asked Pavel.

"This was not so very difficult," said Pavel.

"But how?"

"By telling her I was a writer with a story to sell," said Pavel. "Publishers, editors—a very gullible species. You just have to tell them a story they want to believe is true."

"Christ, I wrote it only because it wasn't true," said Conner. "Not so that I could make it true."

"I wouldn't be so sure," Dex said. "In my experience, every criminal would be an artist if he had the talent, and every artist would become a criminal if he had the guts; in my case, it took an artist to teach me how to be a criminal."

"And what's that supposed to mean?" asked Conner.

Dex gazed out the window. Traffic was light on the Kennedy Expressway. The lights of the city beckoned before they disappeared into the blackness as the train sped east, then downward into the tunnel that led to the Chicago Loop. In that tunnel, the sounds of the train became louder; the wheels screeched and the interior lights flickered onto the faces of Dex, Pavel, and Conner; they were now the only people left in the car. As was the case on Conner's airplane, only reflections were visible in the windows and when Conner saw his reflection, he wasn't sure he knew the person he was seeing anymore.

Dex turned back to Conner. "Look," he said, "when we first met, Conner, you asked me a question and I believe I responded more rudely than I should have."

"What was the question?" asked Conner.

"You asked me how I made my money, and I told you in so many words that it was none of your damned business. Do you remember that conversation?"

"I do," said Conner. "But in a way, you've already told me the answer."

"That's not exactly true," said Dex. "You don't know the whole story."

"Which is what?" asked Conner.

"Well," said Dex, "you know how I've made some of my money. You know about a few million of it, and you might have some ideas about how I made a good deal more. But there was a time when I was clean, as the saying goes. I was out of this 'business' that you and I now find ourselves in. There was a time when I could say I was only an amateur reader and a professional businessman."

"What business?"

"Doesn't really matter. It was never particularly dramatic or interesting or glamorous, and it tended to change from year to year. I bought some things. I sold some things. I invested. Usually, I made money. But it was all legal, every bit of it, that's the point. I had retired from 'crime,' as you might call it. I had been retired for nearly thirty years."

"What happened? Did you run out of money?"

"Not at all. But something did happen."

"What was that?"

"I read a book called *Devil Shotgun*," said Dex.

Conner snorted.

"It's true," said Dex. "The robberies in that book? So well wrought, the details so perfect that I couldn't believe everyone reading it wouldn't try to commit them. I couldn't believe the author himself hadn't tried."

"You're full of shit," said Conner.

"Am I?" Dex reached into his inner pocket and pulled out an old newspaper clipping. The headline read, LIFE IMITATES FICTION: DARING HEIST SEEMINGLY INSPIRED BY CRIME NOVEL. Conner swallowed hard. He tried to read the article, but couldn't focus on the words, kept reading the same sentences over and over. He had heard those rumors of a New Jersey heist that had been inspired by *Devil Shotgun*, but he hadn't given them much credence. He didn't really imagine that any book, particularly any book he had written, could inspire anyone to commit a crime. He wondered if he truly understood himself—perhaps Dex knew him better than he did. Maybe the reader understood more about a book than its writer ever did. Maybe you know more about me from reading this sentence than I ever could.

"You see?" Dex told Conner. "Now you know *The Embargoed Manuscript* wasn't the first work of yours that inspired me."

"How do I even know that's true?" asked Conner.

Dex shrugged. "I could show you a few keepsakes that would prove it to you, but there's little need for that."

"Why?" asked Conner.

"Because you already know I'm being honest."

Conner sighed. He felt sorry he'd come to Chicago. He'd accomplished nothing other than confirming his suspicions and aggravating his anxieties. He wanted to go home. He wanted to see his wife and son. He wanted to sleep. He wanted to move on with his life. He wanted to cash his check and forget everything and everyone, go somewhere far away—just like Salinger.

After the train stopped underground at Washington Street, Conner could barely steady himself to follow Dex and Pavel into the station. He felt his guts grumble. Small, clear bubbles swirled before his eyes. Sometimes he saw double. He walked behind the men as they climbed the stairs and stepped out into the Loop, so much more desolate and sinister than New York at night. They walked past the now-extinguished signs of theaters, department stores with darkened windows, deserted parking garages; a park that was far more black than green at this hour; a lone busker with an open guitar case, strumming a Joni Mitchell song—"Coyote." They walked in and out of the streetlights' amber spill until they neared the lake. The lights of the Navy Pier Ferris wheel blinked on and off, indifferent.

When they reached 680 N. Lake Shore Drive, the doorman greeted Conner by name—"Good to see you again, Mr. Joyce." By now, Conner's mind must have been playing tricks on him, because he could have sworn the doorman was wearing a brass nameplate that read PYNCHON. How old would Thomas Pynchon be now, he wondered. About the same age as this guy. But this was madness; this was the world turned inside out.

Conner followed Dex and Pavel, recalling with specificity the lobby's marble floors, its gaudy chandeliers, the mirrored elevator that led up to the penthouse, the front hallway of Dex's apartment with Norman Mailer's bullet hole, the beautiful library with its view onto the lake, the locked glass bookcase behind which several dozen manuscripts were alphabetically arranged. The authors' names were clearly visible, handwritten on the spines—Capote, Dudek, Hetley, *Joyce*.

Dex took a seat at the head of his library table. Conner remained standing. Pavel stood sentry in the doorway.

"So, do you really give a shit about the books, or is that just an act?" Conner asked Dex.

"You're demeaning your own talent," said Dex. "Great literature inspires me, motivates me. I told you that. I love these books, every one of them. I love each sentence in them."

"That's why you keep them?" asked Conner. "For 'love'?"

"In part, yes," said Dex. "I keep them because of the love they inspire in me and because of the fond memories they provoke, and . . ."

"And?"

"And even if I didn't, I would also need to keep them as security and as evidence."

"Evidence? Meaning what?"

"*Meaning* that if you, or for that matter any other author who works for me, violates the agreement we have made, then I know certain individuals who would be very interested in the books you have written, and I would not hesitate to bring your book to their attention. One day, Margot Hetley will learn that. And if you violate our contract, so will you."

"Go to hell," said Conner.

"Look, Conner," said Dex, "you've been very well paid, better than you ever have been in your life. You delivered your side of the bargain; I've delivered mine. May I give you some advice?"

"I'll pass."

"Well, here it is, nonetheless. Go back to Pennsylvania. Go home to your wife and son. Deposit your check. Forget this ever happened. Forget you ever met me or Pavel. Nothing connects you to the robbery—only one manuscript that no one, save myself and Pavel, will ever read."

"And a flash drive," Conner said.

Dex looked to Pavel.

"*Thees* was my idea," said Pavel. "A keepsake. A memento."

157

"I trust you've disposed of it by now," Dex told Conner. "Will you be staying at the Drake tonight?"

"I want to go home," said Conner.

"Understandable," said Dex. "But if you change your mind, there's a room reserved there. Feel free to use it. The accommodations are much nicer than the ones your publisher pays for, or should I say the ones your publisher *used to* pay for. I've made the reservation under a name that I think you like to use as well."

"Which is what?" Conner asked.

"You don't need me to tell you that," said Dex.

31

The last flight to LaGuardia had already left. So Conner did wind up taking the room Dex had reserved. From the window, he could see nearly half of Chicago. He could see the red and white lights of cars zipping up and down Lake Shore Drive against the black backdrop of Lake Michigan. He could see the expanse of darkness that was Lincoln Park Zoo, where, somewhere inside, a lone coyote on a slab of gray rock was probably howling. Conner felt like howling too—he wished he had someone to share this room with; it was wasted on him. But Dex was right; it was certainly comfortable. And yes, it did seem as if Dex had been right about most things. As far as the advice Dex had given to Conner—go home, pretend nothing had happened, deposit his check, move on with his life— Conner couldn't say for sure whether Dex was right or wrong, but he figured he had no other choice.

"I was going to pretend none of it ever happened," Conner told me. "I wrote a book. Someone committed a crime. There was no connection. That's the choice I made. But I didn't realize a choice had already been made for me."

Conner went to bed past midnight. He had been planning to wake up early to catch the 6:15 a.m. flight, but he still wanted to talk to Angie. He called her on her cell phone; he figured she was probably asleep, but he would leave her a message, apologizing for having lost his temper. He would tell her that he loved her and would see her soon.

Voice mail usually picked up after three or four rings, but this time, Conner heard a click after Angie's phone had rung only once. She picked up.

"I read the *Times*, Conner. You're a fucking liar," she said, then hung up.

Conner tried to call back, but she wouldn't pick up however many times he called, however many messages he left.

"Holy fuck," I said.

"Yep, that's about the size of it, dude," said Conner.

"So, what did you do?"

"The only thing that made sense."

"What was that?"

"I went looking for you."

The rent-a-cop in the drive-in was now laying on his horn and flashing his lights, which was all right because I had to get home, and Conner had told the whole story—at least, all that he knew up to this point. He was on his way back to Pennsylvania, where he would have to talk to Angie. Somehow, she had discovered what he had done, and now he could either gamble his marriage by continuing to try to lie to her, or he could risk everything by telling her the truth.

"You know I trust you, man. You know that by now, don't you?" Conner said to me.

"Yeah. You've told me."

"So, what would you do in my position?"

"You mean tell Angie or not?"

I considered. What would *I* do? Actually, I had a pretty good idea of just what I would do. But I didn't think Conner meant to ask me what I personally would do; I thought he meant to ask what I would do if I were *him*. For myself, I would have done whatever led to my desired outcome, regardless of whether it was the right thing or not. As long as it kept my family together, I probably wouldn't have given a damn about right or wrong. Sign this contract, agree to this or that, who gave a damn as long as it paid our expenses and kept us out of trouble. I hadn't even told Sabine about my conversations with Conner because she probably would have told me I was wasting my time when I should have been working on my own writing. But I figured Conner didn't see me as that sort of person; he saw himself reflected in me, and so I told him what I figured he wanted to hear, what I thought Conner Joyce would do.

"I'd tell her the truth," I said.

"That's what you would do?" he asked.

"It's what Cole Padgett would do," I said.

"What about Conner Joyce?"

"Him too. Even more so."

"Even if it meant I might lose everything?"

"If you don't, what do you have left?" I asked.

It was a bullshit line, corny as hell, but Conner smiled thoughtfully, then cupped my shoulder with one hand. "I knew you were a decent human being," he told me.

"Maybe, maybe not."

He laughed; he must have figured I was joking or being modest, and I didn't see the purpose of telling him I wasn't.

We shook hands and said good-bye. I wished him safe travels back to Pennsylvania and good luck. The high beams of the rent-a-cop's truck were still shining as I watched Conner get back into his rental car, then drive out of the parking lot of the Starlite Drive-In heading north toward Indianapolis. I hooked a left and headed south. As I sped along the dark highway, I had the sensation I was being followed. But by the time I got back home, I couldn't see any cars behind me.

32

I knew I would hear from Conner again soon—far sooner, in fact, than I wanted. But when I did, he was far away from my mind. My own future was my concern, not his, and I didn't have any sense that the two were linked. Part of my mind was in Indiana, part of it was in Chicago, part of it was floating just about everywhere in the United States; if any of my mind happened to be thinking about the Pocono Mountains, I certainly wasn't aware of it. Because now it really looked as though Sabine, the kids, and I would have to leave Indiana.

Although one could not say Sabine's tenure appeal had gone well, it certainly did not go poorly in the way we might have expected. There was more to the story than the vague sensations of disgruntle-ment we felt as we packed up boxes with the intention of moving to my mother's apartment in Chicago or Sabine's parents' house outside Rastatt, Germany, where we would hunker down and figure out what to do next. The university had denied Sabine's appeal, citing some crappy student evaluations and "unsatisfactory service to the department," the latter of which meant that she was axed in part for wanting to spend time with her kids as opposed to hot-tubbing with "Spag" Getty and the members of his reggae band, or attending the semiannual, adults-only departmental outings to one of the local crap-ass wineries. No mention at all was made in the university's report of our Buck Floomington blog.

Sabine was fatalistic about the whole matter; she was German and fatalism was in her DNA. She had no interest in a protracted debate, and certainly didn't want to blow what little savings we had on a doomed legal battle. But I was unwilling to accept the university's decision. So I spent hours, when I wasn't cooking, vacuuming, doing laundry, driving my kids back and forth to Wonderlab, the Indianapolis Zoo, and the Children's Museum, researching successful tenure lawsuits and e-mailing pro-bono attorneys from the university's law school. I was dismayed by my apparent impotence, and began to feel like that line Conner quoted from the John Le Carré novel, but twisted all around:

If you had the opportunity to act like an entitled asshole in order to get what you want, would you take it?

Absofuckinglutely.

That's not the answer I would have given Conner Joyce, but it worked well enough for me.

The outdoor farmers' market was one of my favorite aspects of Bloomington, one of the only reasons to get out of the house before noon on a Saturday—Amish families selling cheese and strawberries; little kids shaking noisemakers to Hoagy Carmichael tunes sung by a husband-and-wife duo who called themselves the Hoosier Hotcakes; barrels of paw-paws for sale. I knew all the salespeople by the products they sold—there was Earnest Swiss Chard Guy, Jolly Hydroponic Basil Dude, Homemade Barbecue Man, Italian Pastry Mom, Earthy Mushroom Lady, and, of course, Dreadlocked Hottie at the Tamale Cart.

Ramona was with Sabine at the library and I was pushing Beatrice's stroller by the acoustic music stage, where a bluegrass step dancing group called Fiddlin' Feet was playing. I was helping Beatrice out of the stroller so that she could get a better view of the stage when I noticed Dr. Lloyd Agger approaching. My wife's current department chair was a bald, muscular man, who, with every confident step, seemed bent on proving that adage about hair loss being evidence of virility. He was known for having five daughters and beating the shit out of all their husbands in one-on-one hoops and squash. Strutting in his khaki shorts, his white T-shirt with BLOOMINGTON UNITED IN DIVERSITY printed in rainbow letters, and his flip-flops, he grinned at me, extended a hand, and asked how Sabine's and my job searches were going.

I smiled back, shook his hand, tried not to wince at his anaconda grip, and told him they were going as well as they could. Fiddlin' Feet was playing the Bob Wills tune "Take Me Back to Tulsa (I'm Too Young to Marry)" and Beatrice was slapping a pair of sticks to keep time with the music.

"I'm sorry this story didn't have a better ending," Agger told me, and in response, I offered some bullcrap about how the end of one story could be seen as the beginning of another, and there was always another chapter to be written.

"That's the writer in you." He laughed and slapped me on the back. "I like that attitude. It should get you far."

I thanked him for complimenting my attitude, but told him my statement was true. Now that the tenure appeal process had been exhausted, I could focus on some opportunities I hadn't been able to take advantage of before. For example, I said, though I had felt angry when I learned that Duncan Gerlach had discovered our Buck Floomington blog entries, then leaked them to members of my wife's department, I was ultimately thankful because I had never realized how strong they were as pieces of writing. "It's amazing how sometimes you can do your best work when you're not even trying," I said.

Dr. Agger was still smiling, although now it appeared as if it was taking him some effort to keep doing so. Perhaps he was reminded of that Buck Floomington line I had written, describing him as a "penis in flip-flops." Either way, I had his attention and so I kept going.

"In fact," I added, "I think you'll find this interesting, Lloyd: I took the liberty of showing the blog to a friend who works in development at HBO. She practically flipped over it; she couldn't stop laughing."

"Flipped?" Dr. Agger asked.

"Yeah, that's the word she used—'I'm "flippin'" over these.' She told me she thought they could go viral."

"Viral?"

"Yeah, viral." I said I was already developing a pilot for a *Buck Floomington* TV series and the characters would be based on individuals from the university, something I could have never done if Sabine and I had been planning to stick around.

"Of course, there'll be that usual disclaimer about, 'any resemblance is purely coincidental,' but nobody ever believes that anyway." I forced out a chuckle.

Unfortunately, this wasn't true in the slightest. But Lloyd Agger, perhaps because he was solipsistic enough to believe HBO would actually be interested in developing a TV series about the inner workings of a graduate school of foreign policy, seemed to have no idea I was putting him on.

"You know that anything written on a university computer becomes property of the university," he said.

"So I guess you may just have to sue me," I said. Agger stalked off to patronize Jolly Hydroponic Basil Guy while I took a seat on the ground beside Beatrice and watched Fiddlin' Feet.

Within weeks, Sabine was offered the opportunity to teach at the university for an additional year, during which she could search for another job, while I was offered an adjunct gig teaching creative writing at $8,000 per semester in exchange for signing a document asserting I would not write anything impugning the reputation of any employees of the university—a document I might be flagrantly violating this very moment. Oh, well.

The extra time, however, proved a mixed blessing. On the one hand, it alleviated some of the existential panic Sabine and I had been experiencing, but our lives didn't become any more pleasant. There were the dirty looks we received in the produce section of the Bloomingfoods natural grocery store, the whispered conversations about us at the arts events we attended, the murmurs of "tenure denied" and "HBO series" we heard in the children's section of the Monroe County Public Library. Even my barber, Kemp, at the Boomerang Hair Salon seemed to have figured out I was a dick. Our daughters stopped getting invitations to playdates from all but a couple of friends, and those were from families that weren't associated with the university. We spent less time together than ever. Sabine was jetting around the country, conducting informational interviews with the Rand Corporation and with think tanks and universities, while I sold as many of our belongings as I could on eBay and Craigslist, procrastinated grading my students' stories, and putzed around with a TV pilot called *Buck Floomington*, which I actually did draft and send to my old Chicago pal Gina, who was developing a show for FX, not HBO, and who told me what

I expected—no one gave a damn about the struggles of professors and house husbands in south central Indiana.

Frequently, on weekends, I would take Ramona and Beatrice to Chicago, where we were helping my mom box up her belongings in preparation for her move to a retirement facility in the North Park Village Nature Center. Her memory was fading, emptying out, and walking the stairs to her second-floor apartment was becoming harder. On one of those Chicago trips, Conner reappeared.

33

It was early March. Sabine was in Washington, DC, sleeping on the couch of her grad-school housemate Rhiannon Nakashima, who now worked for the Center for Public Integrity, and was giving her the lowdown about the grim jobs scene in the nation's capital. In my mom's apartment in Chicago, Beatrice and Ramona were on the living-room couch with my mother, who was trying to interest them in *Last Year at Marienbad*—a film she likes because it's a puzzle without a solution. Meanwhile, I was, yet again, snooping for information about my father, but Mom had either already thrown it all out or boxed it away. Or she simply didn't have anything to hide anymore. I learned from her that secrets were phenomenally easy to keep if you actually wanted to do so. So I simply filled boxes with books and clothes for her move. I could say more about my mother here, describe our conversations in more detail or something like that, but given what happened after I published *Nine Fathers*, you know I won't do that.

I was leashing Hal, preparing to take him for a walk around the neighborhood, when I heard my telephone's "Fables of Faubus" ring. I looked at the display: CONNER JOYCE.

"Where're you going, Dad?" Ramona asked.

"Just walking the dog," I said.

I closed the door behind me and walked out with Hal.

"Hey, dude," I said into the phone.

"Hey, pal." Conner's voice sounded weak and scratchy.

"You OK?" I asked.

"Been better, been worse. At least I'm alive," he said.

"You sound like that was in doubt," I said.

"It was," he said. "Maybe it still is, who knows? Where're you at?"

He coughed, wheezed, then cleared his throat. In the background, I heard chatter and the whirrs and beeps of machines.

"Where're *you* at?" I asked.

"Just getting out of the hospital," he said.

"Which?" I asked.

"Northwestern."

"In Chicago?"

"Yeah. What about you? Where are you?"

"Chicago too."

"Cool. You got some time?"

"A little. Not too much. I'm here with my kids. You OK, man?"

"For now. I think so. But I gotta head out soon."

"Where to?"

"I'll tell you when I see you," said Conner. "And when I do, you might just get that opportunity we've been talking about, pal."

"Who do I get to be?" I asked. "The hero or the decent human being?"

"Same as always. You get to choose."

34

I knew this city better than any other city in the world. I was born here; I grew up here, went to college here, worked writing news copy for the radio station, drove the CBS Radio company car to press conferences all over the city and suburbs. I wrote travel articles about Chicago, met my wife here, set my first and only novel in the neighborhood where my mom still lived—in the drabbest part of the north side, a neighborhood of alleys, walk-ups, gas stations, convenience stores, graveyards, dentists' offices, and strip-mall Asian restaurants and karaoke bars. I knew all this city's weird little alcoves and hiding places, every untraveled forest preserve, where serial killers stashed their bodies, every unlicensed restaurant that masqueraded as a "social club." I asked Conner if he wanted me to suggest some out-of-the-way place to meet where we wouldn't be discovered, but he said that didn't matter anymore.

"Fuck it. Let's just meet at the Coq d'Or," he said.

"Hiding in plain sight?" I asked.

"Something like that." He spat out a rueful laugh, which quickly became a hacking, tubercular cough.

"Are you sick?"

"Nah," he said. "I wasn't in the hospital for the cough."

"What were you in for?"

"I'll explain it all when you get here, bro. How long do you think it'll take you?"

"Twenty minutes? Half an hour?"

It actually took longer. I took side streets most of the way, the same basic route I used to take riding the 50 bus to get to class at UIC. The closer I got to the Drake Hotel, the more slowly I drove. I had the strange sensation I was being set up—for what, I didn't know. Here was my opportunity to either become a hero or demonstrate I was a "decent human being." It was the sort of opportunity the Conner Joyces of the world leaped at, but that I had been avoiding all my life. I didn't give a crap about being a hero or a decent human being. I just wanted to survive.

Along my way, near the corner of Ashland Avenue and Division Street, I stopped to let a coyote cross the street. Conner liked these animals and may have seen great significance and symbolism in the figure of the coyote, but there were actually lots of them in Chicago now. The city had recently initiated its so-called Coyote Project, introducing about three hundred of them to combat the rat population. The coyote crossed slowly, then stopped and stood in the beam of my headlights. I looked into the animal's gray eyes. From the backseat, Hal whined. The coyote disappeared into an alley, and I drove on.

When I got to the Coq d'Or, it was much as I remembered it. If I used to go there to breathe the air my father had inhaled and exhaled when, one night, he met a cocktail waitress and invited her up to the room where I was conceived, by now, I had lost my curiosity. I now knew, no matter how hard I looked, some secrets would never be revealed, as if they were the contents of some strange private library that would be destroyed the moment its owner died. The bar was just a bar; Sidney J. Langer was just a man; my mother had secrets and her own reasons for keeping them—so be it. What difference did any of it make?

"Partner!" Conner said when he saw me. He was sitting at a table by the bar when I arrived, in the most crowded part of the lounge. He had a good view of the pianist who was playing Dave Brubeck's "Take Five." Normally, when Conner greeted me, he stood up, shook my hand, or slapped my back and kissed my cheek; not this time.

"What the hell happened to you?" I asked.

A bandage was wrapped around his wrist, and his right arm was in a sling. His face was clean-shaven and pale; he had lost more weight. There was gray in his hair, shocks of it near the temples. I imagined if I walked out the door and came back a few moments later, Conner's seat would be occupied by an old man. His back would be hunched, his hair silver, and he would carry a hand-carved walking stick with a yellow-eyed falcon for a handle.

I ordered a club soda, and while I waited for it to arrive, I told Conner about the ordeal Sabine and I had been going through in Indiana, the uncertainty we faced, not knowing where we would be living next. I spoke as if I were letting Conner in on a secret and as if he were one of the few people I could trust with this information, and I'm sure part of that was true. But I'd be lying if I said that was my only motivation; I had become a sort of accomplice to Conner's story, and I felt entitled to some dough. Aside from that, it felt good to tell Conner my story—he really seemed to care. "Harsh," he kept saying. "No way," and "Oh, that's bullshit, man."

"So, how'd it all go?" I asked him when I was through.

"Which part do you mean?" he asked.

"Well, your trip back to Pennsylvania, for starters. The last time I saw you, you were heading to Indy to catch a flight home to see Angie. She had called you a 'fucking liar,' I recall."

"Oh yeah," Conner said with a cough, a laugh, and a wistful shake of the head. "Well, that didn't go all that well now that you mention it."

After the drive-in movies, he had gone to Indianapolis. He spent the night there, and in the morning he caught the first plane to LaGuardia. He found Angie's old motorcycle where he had parked it, and rode back to Pennsylvania as fast as the speed limit allowed. He had an inescapable premonition that she had already packed her bags and taken their son. When he and Angie had purchased the home in the Poconos, he had delighted in its isolation. He had figured Atticus would enjoy all those aspects of country life that he'd loved as a boy visiting his grandparents' house in Yardley, Pennsylvania—chasing frogs and fireflies, playing mumblety-peg with a Swiss Army knife. But this time, as he rode west on I-80, he hated every mile, wished he'd never left the city. In fact, he wished he'd never gone to Chicago at all, not the first time he'd met Dex, and not the second time when he'd flown back to confront him.

As it turned out, Conner's fears had been well founded, though the scene at home wasn't quite as dramatic as he'd imagined. Angie was, in fact, leaving; she had packed her bags; she was taking Atticus with her; but she hadn't gone yet.

35

How the hell did you get this, Conner?" Angie was standing by the counter in their kitchen—the beautiful new granite counter in their beautiful, newly renovated kitchen, paid for with the money that Dex had paid Conner. She was wearing jeans and a black leather jacket, and she was twirling a set of keys on a finger as Atticus slept in the carrier strapped to her chest.

Conner didn't need to ask Angie what she was referring to; it was right there on the kitchen counter. It looked battered and stained from the ride in the toilet, but the jewels and MAH monogram were still there, and it was sitting atop the *Times* article about the theft. He had been a fool to flush the damn thing in this old house where the plumbing never worked right. Moreover, he had been a fool to lie to the woman he loved, to the woman who had told him she hated liars more than anything else in the world.

"Angie, I just can't tell you," he said.

There are some people whose beauty is revealed through anger, whose loveliness is accented by flushed cheeks, flared nostrils, piercing eyes, crimson earlobes. Not Angie, Conner said. He followed her around the house as she packed clothes into bags, zipped up suitcases, lugged them outside, and threw them into the trunk of their Subaru.

"I just can't talk about it. I told you," he said as Angie slammed down the trunk of the car, then told Conner to keep his voice down so that he wouldn't wake Atticus. Such had become her modus operandi during arguments. She would raise her voice, then criticize him when he did the same thing.

"Bullshit," she told him.

"It's true. I signed a confidentiality agreement."

"With who?" she asked.

"Hollywood. I told you."

"Hollywood who?"

"Look, Angela, I did nothing wrong." Now he was following her up the stairs and into their bedroom, their beautifully repainted bedroom—avocado-green with eggshell-colored molding. Angie scanned the room to make sure she hadn't forgotten anything.

Conner kept talking. "If I even mention it to anybody and they find out, I have to give back what they paid me," he said.

Angie hustled down the stairs. "If they find out? What? You're telling me somebody bugged this place?"

"I don't know," said Conner.

"You think somebody bugged you?"

"Maybe. I just don't know."

He looked around the house and imagined the whole place was wired. Why not? Everywhere was a good place to conceal a mike or camera. Who knew where surveillance devices could be hidden in a sprawling old house like this, with its cracked walls and its bad plumbing. Conner's mind reeled back to consider everyone who had ever done work in the house; every single person became suspicious—plumbers, painters, carpenters . . . He thought about dog walkers, delivery people, and mail carriers, and considered whether there could be any profession better suited to spying than mail carrier, so blandly noticeable as to seem invisible. He imagined a husky, middle-aged Pavel reeking of vodka and aftershave, arriving at the house one day, claiming to be a contractor, just as he'd managed to get into Shascha's office to snag the flash drive by pretending he was a writer with something to sell. Conner looked at every appliance he owned, every wire he could see—he looked at the baby monitors Angie was disconnecting and throwing into a duffel bag. A bug could be just about anywhere. He wished he had one of those nifty debugging devices that appeared in an early draft of one of his novels before Angie told him to remove it because the NYPD didn't have room in its budget to buy that sort of high-tech gear. He tried to explain his addled frame of mind to Angie, but now Atticus was awake and crying and hungry, and Angie was saying, "Goddammit, Conner, didn't I tell you to keep your voice down?"

And so, despite the heat he felt on his cheeks and the tears burning in his eyes, despite the fact that his entire world was disintegrating before him, he tried to keep his voice down.

36

Atticus was asleep again, and Angie was carrying him as she and Conner made their way down the rocky path to the banks of the Delaware River, where, several lifetimes ago, Conner had built a wooden bench big enough for three. Some of his fondest memories with Atticus and Angie took place here, looking out at the rippling water and the trees beyond it. As the sun dipped behind the dense black-green forests of Pennsylvania, the sky appeared lavender and the orangey-red trees looked as though they were on fire. The beauty of the view hurt; so did Angie's beauty as her anger dissolved into somber resolution. Her newly calm demeanor bespoke certainty; she had made her decision, and when she looked at Conner, it was as though she were watching a memory.

"And this novel of yours?" she asked when he was done explaining. "Where is it supposed to be now?"

"I told you. Dex has it. There was only one copy of the manuscript. That's how he wanted it."

"Christ, Conner." She gazed at him as if the person she loved the most had become the thing that she most dreaded. She had spent a decade in the NYPD being bullshitted by criminals and her superiors, and had spent another decade coaching Conner on how to write that sort of dialogue and make it more believable. She couldn't fathom that he was trying to use the skills she'd taught him against her. "Please don't bullshit me anymore," she said.

"I'm not."

She shook her head. "Then why don't you tell someone else your story? Someone else besides me."

"You mean like a cop?" he asked.

"You got it, CJ," said Angie.

"Ange, they'd never believe me," said Conner.

"You know what?" Angie said. "Neither do I."

"You should have told her about me," I said to Conner as we sat in the Coq d'Or.

"Yeah, maybe. I thought about that, but that just would've made it worse," he said. "I keep it from her and I tell some guy in Indiana she barely even knows?"

"So, she was right. You were lying to her even then."

"Not lying," said Conner. "Just not saying everything."

"Isn't that the same thing?"

Conner considered. "Maybe it is," he said.

37

Conner didn't try to make Angie stay. In the gathering darkness, he sat on his porch swing and watched her drive the Subaru Outback that contained his entire life toward the highway. He went back into the house to get a sleeping bag so he could sleep in the woods; he didn't care how cold it was, he didn't want to spend the night in the house.

Angie had said she was driving back to the city to stay with her mom. He figured he would give her a couple of days to calm down. Then he would try to tell her the story again and make her believe it. But during the time he spent by himself, he felt less inclined to believe that story. Everything that had happened suddenly seemed like a fiction he had dreamt up for Dex. He still had the MAH flash drive to prove the story was true and that he hadn't imagined it, but that didn't matter much. The ride in the

180

toilet had permanently damaged the drive; when he tried plugging it into the USB port of his computer, an error message appeared on his screen.

He spent days brooding, considering, reconsidering, wondering if he should call the police and then wondering how he could possibly do something as foolish as make that call. He wondered if he should do anything he could to get Angie and Atticus back or if he no longer deserved to be with them. He wondered why he had honored his contract with Dex but violated the one he had with Angie.

When enough time had passed for Conner to fool himself into thinking Angie might have forgiven him or would at least be willing to talk, he rode the motorcycle into the city. He deposited his final check. He loitered in front of police stations, even the Twenty-Fourth Precinct, where he had first met Angie. He considered making a confession, but couldn't go through with it.

From the precinct headquarters, he wandered all the way up Amsterdam Avenue to 145th Street, remembering the walks and rides he and Angie had taken when they were young and in love, when they would have done anything to spend just one more moment together. He stood outside the grimy walk-up where he had once waited for her to come running down. He buzzed her apartment, heard Angie's mother's voice on the intercom—she sounded older than he had remembered. When he asked if he could come up, Gladys De La Roja said no, her daughter was not there. The first time, he left a message; the next time, he didn't. He returned several times throughout the day and the evening, but each time he buzzed the apartment, he got the same response—"No, Conner, she's not here, but I'll tell her you came by." She never invited him up, not even to see his son.

Conner wandered through the city, amazed at how many people

he could see and still feel so empty. He kept waiting for Angie to call. He kept checking his phone to make sure that it was charged, and that he hadn't shut off the ringer. But when the phone did ring and Conner picked up, he didn't hear Angela's voice.

"What is it?" Conner asked.

"You have violated our agreement, sir," said Dex. "We need to talk."

38

Conner agreed to meet Dex and Pavel at the Oyster Bar in Grand Central Station, and as he approached the establishment, Conner couldn't escape the notion that this would be a perfect spot to take out a hit on somebody. All Dex and Pavel would have to do would be to open fire, then blend into the crowds before boarding a train and rolling out of town. He sat down on the bench across from them as they were finishing their meals, and tried to determine whether Pavel was packing a weapon. He probably was. Maybe Dex was too. For all Conner knew, there may well have been a poisoned blade hidden in that walking stick.

As Conner joined the men, he noted their demeanors—Dex's stern, Pavel's more apologetic, yet no more helpful, as if Conner's imminent death was little more than an unfortunate fact he could do nothing to reverse. No one offered to buy Conner a meal or a drink.

"You disappoint me, Conner. Truly, you do," said Dex.

"What're you talking about?" Conner tried to deny that he had violated his contract, but he lost patience with himself even before Dex did. Why tell lies if you could no longer bother to believe them yourself? He had violated the agreement, so what punishment would Dex and Pavel exact? Margot Hetley had violated her agreement and she was still alive.

"Why don't I just pay you back? I still have a lot of the money," said Conner. "I haven't spent it all. Far from it."

But Dex knew all about that. "Yes, that is true about the money," he said. "You have spent only perhaps fifteen percent of what we have paid you."

Pavel nodded. "Fifteen percent, sixteen percent, yes, something like *thees*."

"But that sixteen percent would be difficult for you to get a hold of quickly," Dex said. "And the contract does stipulate that the money be paid back immediately and in full."

"Or else what?" Conner asked.

"Do you really need me to tell you?" asked Dex.

"Yes," said Conner. "Actually, I do."

"Think, Mr. Joyce." All pleasantries were gone, replaced by cold formalities. "You're the writer; you have a far more vivid imagination than I do."

"Is that what you told Salinger?" asked Conner. "Is that what you told Dudek?"

"These were men of their word," said Dex.

Conner was about to ask if Dex was implying he was not a man of his word, but he knew that he wasn't anymore. Yes, there had been a time when he had been that sort of fellow—Eagle Scout,

Navy man, all that—but Dex knew he had changed. Dex had made Conner what he was today, or at least made him see what he had always had the potential to become, what every man had the potential to become, what Angie had seen him becoming. Conner shifted his gaze from Dex to Pavel and back again, the former drinking the last of the juice from an oyster shell, the latter daubing his lips with a white cloth napkin, and he understood once again that Dex was right; he did have a vivid imagination. At that very moment, he could imagine all sorts of horrific punishments.

"Look," Conner said. "This was my deal. You made it with me. I fucked it up. OK. Please, *please*, whatever you do, leave my wife and son out of it."

Dex smiled. "You see," he said. "I told you that you had a better imagination than I. What crime did I commit? The one you wrote. What punishment might I inflict? The one you now imagine. Take the worst you can imagine; that is what will happen."

Conner's anger collapsed into desperation. "But you already know I can't repay you immediately," he said. "Not all at once."

"Then we will need to make another arrangement," said Dex.

"Which arrangement?"

"Listen to your imagination. What does your imagination tell you?"

"Oh, fuck your games," Conner shouted.

"I am not playing a game," said Dex. "I have never been playing a game. I have told you what I wanted and you have played games with me. I will ask you again. What does your imagination tell you?"

There was a steak knife beside Dex's plate. How easy it would be to grab that weapon and plunge it into Dex's heart; how easy it would be to chase down Pavel. The criminals in Conner's novels, even in *The Embargoed Manuscript*, had never wanted or intended to be criminals; they were merely men pushed beyond their limits, men who had begun to believe they had no other choice. Conner had never killed a man; he had never thought he could; but the Navy had taught him how, and his time working the crime beat at the *Daily News* had taught him how easy it was to get away with. One crime—wasn't that what his characters always thought? One crime and you'd never have to pay for it. The trouble came when you got cocky and tried to do more. He could do it, he thought, as long as it meant he could keep his wife and son safe.

But just at that moment, when Conner was contemplating murder in the Grand Central Oyster Bar, an idea occurred to him, an idea he sensed Dex had been leading him to all this while. A volt of understanding surged through him. His eyes brightened slightly and he could see just a bit more clearly.

"Oh," Conner said. "Oh, I get it now."

"Yes," said Dex. "I thought you might."

Dex smiled, and so did Conner.

"You mean another book," said Conner.

Dex nodded.

"Another story of a perfect crime," Conner said.

Pavel smiled too. "Something like *thees*, yes," he said.

"A story that will pay back the money I owe you," said Conner.

"Yes, that's it exactly," said Dex. "And everything I make over and above that will be yours."

Pavel produced a contract and handed it to Conner, who didn't bother reading it this time, just signed the damn thing and gave it back to Dex. Dex offered to buy Conner a drink, but Conner said no; he wanted to get to work as soon as he could.

"But how could you do that?" I asked Conner in the Coq d'Or, where the pianist was playing "Naima," by John Coltrane. How could he still work for Dex, given everything that happened, given the threats Dex had made?

Maybe, I thought, this was where I came in. Maybe this was where I could prove my decency or my heroism. Maybe he'd had trouble writing another crime novel for Dex; maybe he could no longer stomach the idea of writing a crime he knew would become reality, and now he was going to call upon me to help him because I wouldn't suffer the same moral conflict. Plan a heist, have someone else carry it out, keep the money left over, tell everyone that I had only written a story, so it wasn't my fault—sounded like a good plan to me.

"I imagine it must have been hard," I said.

"What was?"

"Writing a novel for a man like that, I mean, now that you knew who he really was and what he was after. I don't know how you could square it with your principles."

"Maybe that's how it would be for you," said Conner. "For me, it was easy."

"Then what was hard?" I asked.

"Making Dex think it was hard."

Because, Conner explained, he knew exactly the sort of novel he would write, and he knew how it might solve all his problems—getting Dex and Pavel out of his life and bringing Angie and Atticus back into it. He could have everything he wanted as long as he wrote the right sort of novel.

"What sort of novel would that be?" I asked.

"A novel about a crime destined to fail," he said. "I'd write something that looked like the perfect crime, but when Dex and Pavel tried it, they'd get nailed."

As he sat across from the men in the Oyster Bar, Conner tried to keep himself from acting too cocky, tried to pretend he was still furious with Dex and Pavel. He swore at the men, told them he wanted them out of his life and, once he had written this last book, he was through with them. *For good!* He kicked a chair and threw over a few saltshakers before he exited the restaurant. And then he disappeared into the crowds of Grand Central Station as if he had just committed a hit.

39

Writing a novel about a crime that wouldn't pan out was easy enough—Conner had breezed through enough airport crime novels that weren't remotely plausible, and made assumptions about criminals and law enforcement apparently without ever having done any research. Every James Patterson and David Baldacci novel he had skimmed *en diagonale* seemed ridiculous, and so did every episode of *Law & Order* he had ever watched. The hard part was writing a crime good enough to convince Dex it would work. Conner would have to employ his customary level of detail; he would have to provide enough of it to make Dex believe the story, yet at the same time, create a transition from truth to fiction so seamless Dex wouldn't see it happening.

Conner spent his days brainstorming as he walked along the Delaware River or rode Angie's motorcycle over the back roads of the Pokes. He tapped on his manual Smith-Corona, hoping all his bad ideas would lead to a good one. The urgent need to devise an appropriate idea didn't make the process of finding it any easier. Each day, he considered then rejected dozens of scenarios; by the time the first ice storm of autumn arrived, he had generated enough ideas to fill a small library, and he still hadn't settled on one that felt right.

By now he was on speaking terms with Angie again. She let him take Atticus out for walks whenever he came into the city, walks that were always far shorter than Conner would have liked. He didn't tell her about the plan he had hatched, and she didn't advise him to turn himself in to the police. For the time being, she just wanted to keep her distance. Once Conner had written the book that would get Dex and Pavel out of the way, and he figured he could reveal his story to the police without fear of retribution, he would tell her everything.

Before the ice storm hit, Conner took Atticus for a sled ride through Riverside Park, and returned the boy to Angie right after sleet started mixing with the snow. He wanted to get back to the Poconos while it was still safe to drive. But by the time he got on the road, it was already too slippery—as it turned out, he couldn't make it past East Stroudsburg. He exited the highway, sliding and spinning over the asphalt at barely five miles per hour.

He skidded through downtown East Stroudsburg, in search of a bar or coffee shop where he could wait out the storm. He parked on Courtland Street in front of the main branch of the East Stroudsburg Credit Union, which had closed early because of the weather. He was walking past the bank, heading for a sports bar called the Diggity Lounge, when, out of the corner of his eye, he caught sight of his own image in one of the video monitors in the bank's security booth.

Hail pinged against his cheeks as he paused to look at himself on the screen—there were flecks of ice in his beard, shadows under his eyes. He looked gaunt. He then watched the image switch from one of himself to one of snow-dusted Courtland Street to one of an empty teller booth. The TV monitor scrolled through more than a dozen images, all being taken at that very moment by the security cameras in the bank. At the bottom of the screen was a black band with a digital readout of the date and time. But the readout was wrong. Where the time should have been, zeroes were strobing. He wondered what would happen if someone robbed a bank when the date and time were wrong. How would that affect the admissibility of evidence? This may not have seemed like much to base a story on—no doubt the digital readout would be fixed by the time the bank reopened in the morning—but it gave Conner an idea.

He waited out the storm in the Diggity Lounge, eating stale pretzels, drinking flat sodas, and jotting down ideas on napkins before returning home to his typewriter to write. The key, he knew, was not to take the story too fast. No matter how much he ached to finish so he could return to the important business of reuniting with his family and ridding himself of Dex and Pavel, he worked in the same methodical fashion with which he had approached every one of his books. He did not skimp on detail. He wanted to get so many details right that Dex wouldn't be able to recognize the ones he got wrong.

He wrote one thousand words per day and spent the rest of his time revising those words and walking through East Stroudsburg, trying to imbue his novel with the town's ambience. He strived for pinpoint accuracy, particularly when writing about the bank. He included the model numbers of each of its dozen cameras, researched the manufacturing processes used to produce its Mosler security vault. He wrote down the names of each of the bank's security guards, managers, loan specialists, and tellers, whom he greeted every morning when he withdrew cash—so much so that he began to worry the bank's employees might suspect he was planning to rob the joint himself. He introduced himself to Hunter Leggett, the bank's regional manager, gave Leggett copies of *Devil Shotgun* and *Ice Locker*, both now available for 50 percent off, and got a tour of the bank vaults and a crash course in the bank's security systems. He even watched Hunter Leggett type in his own security access codes. It had always amazed Conner how much purportedly confidential information he could get merely by identifying himself as an author or journalist. Without even having to show a business card or pass through a metal detector, he had gotten access to runways at LaGuardia and JFK just weeks after 9/11, had sat seatbelt-less on a day's worth of runs on a Brink's truck, had gotten within easy shooting distance of governors, senators, and even one time the vice president of the United States.

Conner made sure to write a genuine novel, not just a blueprint for a crime. If he wrote only the heist and not the story behind it, Dex might concentrate too fully on the details and come to identify the flaws. So when Conner saw Rosie Figueroa, one of the bank's tellers, alone at the Diggity Lounge one night after the East Stroudsburg Credit Union had closed, he bought her a beer and learned her story—single mom, divorced, undergraduate degree in finance from East Stroudsburg U. She didn't want to talk much about her ex-husband, but Conner was still good at getting people to tell him their stories, and from what the woman said, he was able to concoct a suitable biography for a thief. He imagined Rosie's ex to be a convict just out of the joint, seeking to take advantage of his ex-wife's position at the bank. Rosie's ex-husband would force her to ingratiate herself with the bank's security director, from whom she would learn the pass codes, security protocols, and remote video procedures Conner himself had learned through his research. He called Rosie's husband Chet Davila, a name he picked out of an old phone book.

In the novel Conner was writing, Rosie and Chet conspired to commit a robbery at midnight on February 29. He had chosen the date carefully. During the course of his research, he had learned that the East Stroudsburg bank was protected by two major computer systems, but that each system was manufactured and serviced by a different company. The video cameras were manufactured and maintained by DGA Security Systems in Manhattan. The German-based multinational P. B. G. Krenz, whose American headquarters were located in Tallahassee, Florida, maintained the locks to the doors, the vault, and the keypads. The systems had been installed at different times, and whenever there was some sort of malfunction, which usually took place during a particularly brutal storm, such as the one Conner had experienced when he first concocted his story idea, both systems broke down and Hans Plitsch, the bank's security director, had to coordinate the schedules of repair people from both DGA and Krenz.

The difficulty of coordinating schedules was harder to address if anything happened to go wrong during a leap year on February 29, since DGA and Krenz had different, arcane methods for dealing with the extra day. Every four years, at the end of February, the two systems would stop talking to each other, forcing them to shut down, leaving the bank essentially unguarded, without either functional locks or security cameras during the ten minutes it took the systems to reboot. For those ten minutes between midnight and 12:10 a.m., the only thing keeping a thief—in this case Rosie's ex-husband, Chet Davila, but in real life Dex Dunford and Pavel Bilski—was the overnight security guard, Lyle Evans. Once Pavel and Dex had overpowered Lyle Evans, they would have ten minutes to take everything they could carry.

40

The Coq d'Or's pianist was taking a break and had joined some of the tourists at the bar to watch a college basketball game. The TV didn't seem like it belonged in the bar, which itself conjured up an era before the advent of television. When I used to come here to write, nobody watched sports.

On the TV screen, MARCH MADNESS!!! was flashing in bright red letters. Only a couple of days had passed since February 29, and I hadn't heard anything about a leap-year bank robbery. Then again, I didn't read the newspapers much; when I did, I pretty much stuck to the front page, the sports, the op-eds, the job ads, and the vegetarian recipes in the Dining section. I looked at the gauze and tape around Conner's wrist, the sling he was wearing. Both were bright white, as if brand-new.

"How much of this is true?" I asked.

"The whole story was true," said Conner. "At least up until the part that wasn't."

"When did the story stop being true?" I asked.

"February twenty-eighth."

According to Conner, all the details he had written about the bank itself were accurate; the entire leap-year plot was bulljive. What happened when midnight struck on the second to last night of February? Absolutely nothing. Video cameras continued to run; locks stayed locked; Lyle Evans remained at his security post, and there would have been little chance for Dex and Pavel to "overpower him" as they had in the novel because, unlike the lethargic caricature in the story Conner wrote, Lyle Evans was a big, muscular, conscientious dude. Plus, just in case, about fifteen minutes before midnight, Conner's plan had been to call Lyle Evans and warn him.

Once Conner had completed the manuscript for the novel he had decided to call *Leap of Fate*, the hardest part was waiting—that, combined with the need to suppress whatever desire he had to tell Angie what he was planning. He wanted to tell Dex he had finished, and worried that Dex might not get in touch until after February 29. If Dex didn't get the manuscript in time to act on it, he would either have to wait another four years or write another novel that wasn't so time sensitive.

But Dex got in touch with Conner on the twenty-seventh of January.

"I bet you remember that date, my friend," Conner said to me.

"Why?" I asked.

"That's the same date Mr. Salinger died."

I nodded, pretending I knew.

Conner met Dex and Pavel at the bar of Keens Steakhouse, where he handed over the manuscript of *Leap of Fate*, which he had dedicated to Dex. This was to be a quick meeting, Dex had told Conner over the phone—no meal, no drinks, just a drop-off. At the bar, Pavel regarded the title with his customarily inscrutable amusement.

"Is it a thriller?" Dex asked.

"Yeah, but with a twist," said Conner.

"Yes, with you, always a *tweest*," said Pavel. "I like *thees veddy motch*."

"How long do you think it'll take you to read it?" asked Conner.

Dex flipped through the first few pages, then turned to the last page and read the final paragraph before fixing Conner with a stare.

"You asked when you would hear from me?"

"I did."

"Well, judging from what little I've seen so far," said Dex, "I imagine that you'll be hearing from me on or around the twenty-ninth of February."

Dex packed the manuscript in his attaché case and strolled to the exit, leading the way with his walking stick. Pavel followed behind. "So long, Conner," Pavel said. The way Pavel said "Conner" sounded funny, but it didn't register to Conner until later that he had never heard Pavel use his first name.

41

February 29 took far too long to arrive. Each day seemed to last longer than the one before. Conner tried to pass the time. He worked out—ran ten miles a day, lifted the dumbbells he hadn't used in more than a decade. He repainted just about the entire inside of his house, cleaned it again and again, preparing for what he hoped—no, what he *knew*—would be Atticus and Angie's imminent return. He looked forward to weekend walks and breakfasts with Atticus, who was now able to conduct conversations, albeit brief ones—"Want to go home," he frequently said. Conner read a lot too, actually read all nine volumes of the Wizard Vampire Chronicles series and, to his surprise, got caught up in the stories. No matter how unpleasant an individual Margot Hetley may have been in real life, he couldn't deny she had mad skills. He understood why her work was worth millions, why Dex had recognized "a raw and

ruthless talent" in her before she had betrayed him. What struck
Conner most profoundly about the books was their ferocity and
brutality; Hetley's audience was made up mostly of kids and teens,
and yet there was more bloodletting and perverse sexuality in any
chapter of the Wizard Vampire Chronicles books than in any of
Conner's purportedly adult crime novels. Conner's characters ago-
nized over the crimes they committed; Margot's wizards, vampires,
and vampards never gave a damn.

As the last day of the month approached, Conner didn't know
whether the fact he hadn't yet heard from Dex was good or bad
news. If all went according to plan, he might not hear from Dex
at all, he told himself. Dex would try to enter the bank when midnight struck on the twenty-ninth and the first Conner would learn
of him would be when he saw his picture on the front page of the
Morning Call.

By February 28, Conner still hadn't heard a word. He slept fit-
fully, had trouble eating, left half-finished plates and bowls of food
in the kitchen sink, drank Campbell's soups straight out of the can.
He tried to read but couldn't focus. He tried turning on the TV but
couldn't follow any program, not even sports. He wanted to take a
ride, but he worried about getting into an accident. He wanted to
talk to somebody but knew he wouldn't take out his phone to make
any call until 11:45 p.m., when he would warn Lyle Evans.

Well after night had fallen, the air was cold and damp by the
Delaware River. Conner sat outside on the bench, shivering beneath
a black, star-filled sky. He was occupying himself by wondering
what would happen after it was all over, for he knew this ordeal
would soon end. Someday he would be with his wife and son and
they would be able to look back on all this. Would they stay here
in this house or would they move far away—maybe to Monroeville,
Alabama, or to Cornish, New Hampshire, or even to Mexico City,

where B. Traven had fled? J. D. Salinger was dead, God rest his phony old soul. Maybe there was still a nice empty home in Cornish available for a decent price.

Conner lost himself in these reveries, these lovely fantasies of what his life could and might very well soon become. He felt intoxicated by possibilities when he heard a car approaching his house. He looked at his phone to check the time—it was nearly half past eleven.

Conner made his way to the top of the path. The driveway was dusted with snow. Conner didn't see a car, but his porch light was on and a set of footsteps led up his front walkway to his mailbox. In that mailbox, illuminated by the porch light, was an envelope. Conner took the envelope, ripped it open, and unfolded a letter— *"Conner, I've read your manuscript and we need to discuss revisions as soon as possible. Cordially, Dex."*

Conner looked up from the letter and noticed that his front door was open a crack and there seemed to be a light on inside.

42

Everything inside Conner was telling him to get the hell out, and yet he moved forward. Everything inside Conner was telling him something was going wrong, and yet he tried to act as if the plan were proceeding as it should have. He pushed his front door open all the way and walked through his hallway toward his kitchen, where the fluorescent light was on over the sink. Standing at the counter, drinking water from a black mug, was Pavel. He looked the same as he always did—a husky man in his late fifties in a heavy old sports coat—and yet for those first moments standing before Pavel, Conner couldn't rid himself of the odd sensation that Pavel belonged in this kitchen, while he did not.

"How the hell did you get in here?" Conner asked.

Pavel shrugged. "Doors, locks, *thees* is not so difficult." Pavel finished his water, then placed the mug down in the sink. "So, Conner, are you ready to go?"

"Where?" Conner looked down at the time on his phone—only a few more minutes remained before he was supposed to call Lyle Evans.

"A ride," said Pavel. "Dex is in the car outside."

Conner told himself to play it cool, yet was gripped by foreboding and despair. "The first time I met Dex, we walked, remember?" he said. "You remember what he said? He said if he were in my position, he wouldn't get into a car with a stranger."

"Yes, but we are not so much strangers anymore, Conner," said Pavel. Conner wondered if Pavel knew what awful things were going to happen next, and if by calling him Conner, Pavel was trying to reassure or warn him.

"What if I tell you no?" Conner asked.

Pavel tilted his head from one side to the other, bit his lower lip, inhaled then let the breath out in a loud sigh.

"So," said Conner. "That's the way it is?"

"I am afraid *thees* is true," said Pavel.

"He says he wants to talk about revisions," said Conner.

"*Reveesions*, yes. *Thees* is what he wants to discuss."

"Do you know what those might be?"

Pavel frowned and shook his head. "Dex has his own opinions," he said. "Mine are not so important."

"You read this one too?"

"I enjoyed the manuscript, Conner," said Pavel. "I thought it was quite well done. Perhaps the characters could have been better developed, but the crime was clever, and as always, the details were quite convincing. But this is only my own personal opinion. It does not impact on anything. Come, let us go to the car."

43

A black Crown Victoria was parked in Conner's driveway, motor running, Dex at the wheel. Dex wore a chalky gray suit and a lavender pocket square that somehow managed to contrast well with his shimmering, indigo tie. Conner got into the back of the car and looked at the digital readout on his phone, which matched the time on the dashboard clock. It was a quarter to midnight—no way to call Lyle Evans now.

"So, these revisions?" he asked as Dex steered the car off Conner's property, heading toward Interstate 80. "You didn't ask for any revisions the first time around."

"Yes, that's true." Dex said. "But you must understand that's unusual. With some of my authors, we've had to send the manuscript back and forth a dozen times before we got it right."

"What about Salinger?" asked Conner.

"Him especially," he said. "Very sloppy. I probably let him get away with too much. With you, we got it right the first time. And in this case, I'd say you're almost there; the revisions I'm talking about are quite minor."

"Just minor changes?" asked Conner. "Why do you even bother me about minor changes? Why don't you just make the revisions yourself?"

"But that's not the agreement, Conner," said Dex. "You are the writer. This is your work."

Conner let out a short, thin breath. From the backseat, he looked out through the windshield. The snow was slanting down as Dex pressed on the gas pedal and merged onto the highway, heading east toward New York City. He drove in the right lane, windshield wipers going fast. The highway seemed empty; save for a truck here or there, everyone heading to the city had already made it there. The three men watched the road. For some time, nobody spoke.

"All right," Conner finally said. "What do you need me to do?"

"Well, here's the difficulty." Dex steered the Crown Vic using only two fingers on his right hand, apparently unconcerned by the weather. "I truly am fond of the setup you wrote," he said. "And I do like all the detail. You're very good at that, but you already know that. I like the business about leap years too. I found all that quite original. I think once you switch the characters around a bit, you'll really have something that we'll be able to use."

"Switch characters?" asked Conner. "What does that mean?"

Dex signaled a turn. Conner had expected they might be driving all the way to New York, but now Dex was turning off at the first exit, heading for East Stroudsburg.

"You see, I like the story of the bank teller, Rosie Figueroa," Dex said. "You really captured the way she spoke; but there's something about her that doesn't quite add up. I think you rushed the writing of the story too much. All that business about her ex-husband using her to do a bank job—it's all so convenient and convoluted. I just didn't buy it. I didn't really think Rosie would marry somebody like that, not the way you wrote her. And, even if she had, I didn't believe a character like that ex-husband of hers would be clever enough to come up with the sort of scheme he does. He seemed too simple to know so much about computer systems and video security, and certainly too simple to conceive of a crime of that nature. To tell you the truth, Conner, the crime would seem so much more convincing if it were committed by someone like . . ." Dex's voice trailed off.

"Someone like who?" Conner asked.

"Someone like you, Conner." Dex stopped the car.

The Crown Victoria was now stopped in front of the East Stroudsburg Credit Union. No other car was parked on the street. There were no police cars in sight. The bank looked dark; the only lights emanated from the security booth, where Lyle Evans's face was illuminated in the flashes of video monitors. Conner looked at the clock on the dashboard. It was 11:59 p.m. "What's going on?" he asked.

Dex put the car in park and turned back to face Conner. "It is one minute to midnight," he said. "When sixty seconds pass, it will be February 29. Leap year, you remember. The security systems in the bank will go down; that's what you wrote. They will have ten minutes to recalibrate; that's what you wrote too. For that amount of time, the bank will be 'essentially unguarded.' All you have to do is 'take care of the guard.' Isn't that right? Isn't it as simple as that?"

Conner gazed blankly at Dex, whose eyes looked as pale and unsympathetic as the yellow eyes of the falcon on his walking stick.

"I do not like being fucked with," Dex said. "And I have told you I do not like being lied to any more than you or your wife do. You have ten minutes to do everything you wrote in your novel. If what you wrote was true, then you won't have any difficulty." He turned to Pavel. "Hand Mr. Joyce your gun," he said.

Pavel reached into a shoulder holster and withdrew the weapon that he had handed to Conner back at the Coq d'Or Lounge, the weapon J. D. Salinger once held, the weapon Norman Mailer once fired at Dex's wall. Pavel pressed the gun into Conner's hand, then stepped out of the car and opened the back door.

Conner looked at the clock. It was now midnight. He got out of the car, holding the gun.

"Ten minutes," Dex repeated. "Go."

44

Conner stood on the sidewalk, midway between Dex's Crown Vic and the front door of the bank. He looked at the car. Pavel was standing by the curb, leaning against the car, watching. Inside the bank, Conner could see Lyle Evans at the video monitors. Evans was beginning to stand up and walk to the front door. The security guard was holding a gun in one hand; in the other, he held a bound manuscript.

Conner looked to the bank, then to the car, then to the bank again. He looked up and down the snowy sidewalks and streets. He weighed his options. He weighed the gun. His aim would have to be dead-on—first Dex, then Pavel, and all that before Evans got to the door. That was the choice a Conner Joyce character would have made, not the one he wanted to make, but the choice destiny had forced upon him. He cocked the weapon, took a breath, and aimed. But *fuck*, no, he couldn't. He threw the gun to the ground and ran up Courtland Street. He heard tires spinning in the snow, the screech of a car lurching forward, heard the door to the bank open, heard a gunshot crack through the air. He kept running.

The one advantage of having done so much research about East Stroudsburg while writing *Leap of Fate* was that Conner now truly knew these streets—he knew the alcoves and doorways in the alley behind the Pocono Cinema; he knew each storefront insurance company and travel agency. He knew the curves and drops of Route 209, knew the crisscrossed pathways that led to the quad on the campus of East Stroudsburg University. He knew which classroom buildings were open after dark. The one disadvantage of having written all these details was that now Dex and Pavel knew them too. He may have been the cartographer, but Dex and Pavel had the map. Wherever Conner ran, he saw the approaching headlights of that black Crown Victoria; whenever he stopped to crouch in an alley or behind a Dumpster, he heard two sets of footsteps coming toward him. Moments after he had run inside the Foreign Languages Building of ESU, he heard the front door creaking open. And so he ran again.

He ran over slick white sidewalks and streets, around the gravestones in the Stroud Cemetery. And yet as he ran, questions remained—where could he go; what could he do? His plan was shot. Dex and Pavel were after him, and he didn't know which was more frightening—what would happen if he got away or what would happen if he didn't. He should have fired that gun when he had the chance. He would have done it if he had been a different sort of person; he would have done it if he had been a character he was writing in a novel, where he could eliminate all the anxious adjectives and adverbs he felt—"Cole Padgett fired the weapon. Two bodies were lying on the sidewalk. Dead. But that was OK, because Cole Padgett had no other choice. And now it was time for Cole Padgett to move on."

In the shadows of a stone mausoleum, Conner crouched down and pulled out his phone to call Angie. He felt thankful to hear her voice mail. He told her everything that happened, told her every detail he could remember as if this might be the last chance for her to hear the story, every detail he had left out when he had tried to tell her the story before. He called back every time he had used up his allotted minutes. When he was done, Angie's voice mailbox was full and he was running again, along streets he had crossed before, over sidewalks where he saw familiar shoe prints. He ran over tire tracks that Dex's car had made. He didn't want to go home—he wouldn't be safe there—but he couldn't think of anywhere else to go. He'd get Angie's motorcycle, ride it into the city, turn himself in. "I'm the guy people're looking for, and here's the flash drive to prove it." He wished he could be Cole Padgett, a man who rarely feared taking a chance. He wished he could be Steve McQueen—McQueen on a Suzuki with Devil Shotgun exhaust pipes could outrace any geezer in a Crown Vic. But sadly, he wasn't fictional and he had never been as good on that bike as Angie was.

On the way to Route 611, he stopped to catch his breath at a bus shelter. Taped to the glass was a faded and crinkled flyer advertising Trailways service to Port Authority in New York City. He took note of the bus station address, then started running again.

The Delaware Water Gap station was all but empty and the heat didn't seem to be working. Conner could see his wispy breaths materializing then dissipating before him. The ticket kiosks and snack counter were shuttered. The last bus of the night had already left and there wasn't another scheduled to depart until 4:15 in the morning; but there was a guard on duty, sitting at his security station—a wooden stand that looked like a dais. The guard was wearing a heavy black parka, hood up, and a green New York Jets knit hat. Conner asked him if it would be all right if he waited there until the bus came.

"It's all right with me if it's all right with you," the guard said.

Conner wished he could sleep. Instead, he remained in the pew nearest the security station. He kept focused on the front door, waiting to see if Dex and Pavel were coming. He didn't know what he would do if he saw them—run like hell or instruct the security guard to draw his gun. But after he caught sight of the Crown Vic, which slowed as it came into his view, Pavel and Dex did not emerge from the vehicle; they just drove off. When the Trailways bus pulled up at the station and Conner walked outside to board it, he didn't see any sign of Dex's car.

45

The sun had not yet risen when the Trailways bus merged onto the interstate. Conner had feared Pavel would already be on board, or that he or Dex would get on the bus at the Panther Valley stop, but no one got on there. And though highway traffic got a bit heavier as the bus exited onto I-95 and approached the Lincoln Tunnel, Conner didn't notice any cars that looked familiar.

Conner hadn't packed for this trip. Somewhere in the Poconos was a house full of his belongings. Somewhere in the city he was approaching, he had a wife and son, assuming they were still OK. In libraries across America and in the few bookstores that remained in the country, there were copies of books he had written, stories of imaginary lives he had led. In a private library in Chicago, there was the only copy of a book called *The Embargoed Manuscript*. And in a black Crown Victoria, or in the hands of a bank security guard in the Poconos, was a manuscript called *Leap of Fate*. But as he rode on that Trailways bus, all he had were the clothes he was wearing, a wallet with credit cards, fifty bucks and some spare change, and a flash drive that hadn't been his in the first place. And on West 100th Street at the Twenty-Fourth Precinct, where he went to turn himself in, that was all he had to deliver to Desk Sergeant Mitch Gales, an amiable, potbellied man who looked as if he were approaching retirement age and seemed as if he would have preferred if Conner hadn't shown up at all. The man was watching *SportsCenter* and eating chili out of a Styrofoam bowl. Conner remembered Gales from when Angie had worked there, but Gales gave no indication of remembering him.

"Help ya, buddy?" Gales asked.

"I've got something people are looking for," Conner said, and handed him the flash drive.

The Twenty-Fourth Precinct didn't have much of a lockup, just a bench and a toilet in a room with white-tiled walls and a cracked cement floor lit by fluorescents, whose glare was reflected by the white walls. Conner was the only person in the cell, so there was little to distract him from his doubts and fears, both of which kept growing with every passing moment. He hadn't been in church since his son's baptism, but he prayed hard in that cell, promised to dedicate his life to performing good acts if only Angie and Atticus could stay safe. He offered to give up the hope of seeing them again, if that's what it would take to protect them.

Time passed—who could tell how much. Conner paced his cell. He lost any concept of how many hours were going by—whenever he called out to ask what time it was and Gales told him, the answer surprised him. He had to ask whether it was morning or night, and on two occasions, he guessed wrong. Once he fell asleep and when he awoke, he figured he had been asleep for a whole day, but only a few minutes had passed. He wondered who would come to see him first—the NYPD? The FBI? Shascha herself? He was still pondering these questions when Sergeant Gales unlocked his cell.

"You must be a pretty important guy, Mr. Joyce; you must sell a lotta books." Gales was holding a Ziploc bag with everything Conner had left at the front desk—wallet, phone, and the flash drive, too.

"Yeah, right," Conner said.

"I'm not joking, Mr. Joyce. You're free to go."

What did he mean, Conner asked. Hadn't he called downtown? Hadn't he called the FBI? Hadn't he researched the case?

"Yeah, we looked into all that, everything you told me," Gales said, but he added that he had just gotten a call instructing him to release Conner and to return all his belongings.

"Who called you?" Conner asked.

Gales opened the cell door. "Your friend's here to pick you up," he said.

"Friend?" Conner felt color return to his face, felt all the weariness of the past hours dissipate, replaced by an exhilaration he could compare only to the first rush of love. Angie must have gotten his messages, must have heard all the details he had told her, must have pulled some strings to get him released. He thanked Gales, shook the man's hand twice, then walked out of the cell, sprinting into the lobby where he imagined Angie waiting.

But Angie wasn't there.

46

You are disappointed to see me. I understand. I am sorry for *thees*," said Pavel Bilski. He was now wearing a long, lined khaki trench coat that fit tightly over his blazer. But for all Conner felt, the man might just as well have been wearing an executioner's robe. Every drop of energy and excitement Conner had felt moments before had now bled out of him as suddenly as if his throat had been slit. He made no effort to argue with Sergeant Gales; he knew his cause was futile. Someone had paid Gales off, or had paid somebody else off, probably Dex had done it; it didn't matter. Wherever Pavel was headed, Conner could run or he could follow; either way, he would wind up in the same place. I had once told Conner about a quote from one of my mother's favorite films, and that quote returned to him now as he considered his predicament—*"Oui, je peux perdre, mais je gagne toujours"*—*Yes, I can lose, but I always win.*

Conner followed Pavel out of the precinct headquarters and onto 100th Street, expecting to be blasted with daylight. But it was night. He expected to see Dex outside, waiting in a car. But no one was out front. He remembered how full these streets had seemed whenever he had walked along them with Angie; it seemed significant to him that they were empty now. Empty apartments, empty squad cars, an empty library, an empty church, empty storefronts with For Rent signs in them, buses and taxis without any passengers.

"Where's Dex?" Conner asked Pavel.

"He has flown back."

"Chicago?"

Pavel nodded. He made a gesture, indicating that Conner should walk with him, then started to head west. Conner thought of asking where they were going, but didn't see what difference the answer would have made.

"I assume you're carrying," he said to Pavel, miming a gun.

"*Thees ees* true, yes," said Pavel.

As he walked alongside Pavel, Conner took out his phone to call Angie. The voice mailbox was still full.

"My wife," Conner said. "She's still not answering."

Pavel raised his eyebrows.

"Is she all right?" Conner asked.

"As far as I know," said Pavel.

"Have you seen her?"

"I have not."

"Has Dex?"

"Neither has he," said Pavel, then added philosophically, "as far as I know."

The farther west Conner walked, the darker the streets seemed to become. Past Broadway, every building appeared to be cast in shadows.

"Are we going to someone's apartment?" Conner asked.

"No," said Pavel.

"Are we looking for your car?"

"No, Conner, we are not."

"Are we going someplace to talk?"

"No," said Pavel. "I do not expect there will be much talking after it is done."

Riverside Park was never particularly crowded this far north, especially not at night. Every so often, someone would turn up dead here—a drug deal gone wrong, a homeless person who got killed for someone else's kicks. The park was a good place for a killing; the Hudson was a good place to dump a body. Conner thought back to the time he spent in the Navy, all the things he thought he would have been willing to die for. Now he couldn't imagine dying for his country—his family, though, that was different. Whatever Pavel and Dex had in mind, he would go along with it; he wouldn't fight, as long as Atticus and Angela would be safe.

"Did Dex plot all this out?" Conner asked Pavel.

"Most, yes," said Pavel.

"This walk? Did he plot this walk?"

"He did."

"And did he plot what would happen at the end of it?"

"Yes," said Pavel. "He had a plan for this, too."

"I assume the gun is loaded?"

"Always."

"And that you plan to use it."

"This is the plan."

"I could run," said Conner.

"I would not advise that," said Pavel.

"I could. But I won't. I won't resist if you promise me something."

Pavel stopped walking near a set of stairs that led down to the park's lower level, barely visible at all in the blackness. The river lay just beyond, hard to make out from this vantage point and yet Conner could hear the flow of the water.

"Promise me," Conner repeated, "nothing will happen to my family. Once I'm gone, that's the end of the story. I don't want them to owe Dex anything. I don't want him to take any revenge out on them for something they had nothing to do with."

"I am sorry, Conner, but I am afraid that is not exactly what I have in mind." Pavel drew the gun.

47

Conner had spent a lifetime around guns, and yet this was the first time he had seen at such close range a gun he was certain would be used against him. It looked small in Pavel's hand.

"Pavel? Don't you have a family?" he asked.

"I left them long ago. Much heartache. But familiar story. *Pedestrian*. Not so interesting."

"Isn't there something I can do?" asked Conner.

Pavel held up a finger to quiet Conner. He patted Conner down, as if searching for a weapon. He reached into one of Conner's pockets and took out a pen—the black-and-gold Montblanc that had once belonged to J. D. Salinger. Pavel unscrewed it; inside was a small microphone receiver. Pavel cracked the pen in two, then threw it down, speckling the snow with black ink.

"*Ees* there something you can do?" Pavel asked. "Yes, Conner. There is. Take the gun." The weapon was lying in Pavel's open palm. "Take it," he said.

"That didn't turn out so well the last time," said Conner. "What're you trying to frame me for this time?"

"Frame?" Pavel asked. "Nothing is framed."

"Then what's the twist?"

"The *tweest*? This is it. The *tweest*. In Dex's story, I am supposed to shoot you, you understand."

"Dead?" asked Conner.

"This is it. Exactly. This is what he would like. You dead. The Hudson River, et cetera. He is no writer. His is an obvious story. Unnecessarily crude. Not so imaginative. And then, of course, the next step."

"Which is?"

"Which is I take a cab uptown to your mother-in-law's apartment. I find your wife, your son, and there are some ugly things that I say and do to them there. I do not wish to speak further of this."

Conner made as if to speak. Pavel interrupted. "But I do not like this story so much. I prefer my own way of devising a story. More elegance. Less bloodshed and cruelty."

"What happens in your story?" asked Conner.

"The one I will tell Dex if he finds me?" Pavel shrugged. "I will say that you and I, we struggled for the gun. You grabbed it, you shot me, perhaps in the hand, perhaps in the leg, nowhere too dangerous. You choose. Something like *thees*. It will not seem so implausible."

"But why?" asked Conner.

"Because I do not like to shoot people in general, and I certainly do not want to shoot you, Conner," said Pavel.

"Why not?"

"Perhaps it is because I have a soft spot for writers," said Pavel. "Particularly those who wrote me nice letters many, many years ago."

Pavel reached into the inside pocket of his blazer, from which he extracted a folded sheet of yellowed paper.

"Dear Mr. Dudek," the letter began; it was signed by Conner Joyce. It was one of the many letters Conner had written when he was a young man. He had written to so many of his heroes and role models—Thomas Pynchon, J. D. Salinger, and Jarosław Dudek, the Olympic shot-put medalist and author of *Other People, Other Lives* who had once worked as a functionary for the Ministry of Internal Affairs.

"Dudek?" asked Conner.

"I am he."

Conner studied the man's face; he could see the resemblance to the last known photo of Jarosław Dudek. And he could recognize the sardonic, shrugging, fatalistic humor of Dudek's prose in Pavel's speech too.

"But you disappeared," said Conner.

"I did," said Jarosław Dudek.

"You never published again."

"This I did not."

"And you wound up working for Dex?"

Dudek took a breath and smirked. "In a sense, one way or the other, we all wind up working for Dex," he said.

"But who's Pavel Bilski?" asked Conner.

"*Thees* is the name of a character in a book I once wrote."

"I don't think I read that book."

"Only one man did," said Dudek.

"Dex?"

Dudek nodded.

"So, it's all true. Everything—about Salinger and everyone else."

"Yes," said Dudek. "All true."

"And the flash drive? That was your idea, not Dex's."

"Yes. So one day you would be able to prove your story was true."

Conner looked down at the fountain pen that had concealed the mike. "And that's how?" he asked.

"How what?" asked Pavel.

"How you listened to me? How you knew what I was doing?"

"Yes, of course, but if not that, then something else. There are numerous ways. I have much experience with this. Much professional experience. This is unimportant. We have other business to attend to."

"Like what?" asked Conner.

Pavel reached into a trouser pocket, took a key, and handed it to Conner.

"What's that?" asked Conner.

"Dex's key," said Dudek. "There should be a manuscript or two in his apartment that could be of some use to you."

Conner took the key. "What will I do if Dex is there?"

Dudek shrugged. "He is an old man, Conner. And he has lost his best protection."

"You mean you?"

"This is my meaning—yes."

Conner took the gun. He wanted to ask Dudek so many more questions—about writing, about Poland, about what exactly he had done for the Ministry of Internal Affairs, about how he had spent the past twenty-odd years, about whether or not he would publish again.

"Perhaps we can discuss this upon some other occasion," Dudek said. "But now, it is time for you to shoot me."

"What will you tell Dex if he finds you?" asked Conner.

"A story. He likes stories. This is what I like best about him. Perhaps he will believe me. Perhaps he will not."

"And if he doesn't?"

"I wouldn't worry about me. This is not your problem," said Dudek. "And I have always been quite adept at finding ways to disappear. Now, shoot me, Conner."

Conner took half a dozen steps backward. He cocked the weapon. He aimed it at Jarosław Dudek's leg. And then he fired.

48

The last flight to Chicago was leaving at 10:05 p.m., and Conner had less than an hour to catch it. He had waited in Riverside Park until he made sure Jarosław Dudek had hobbled into a cab to Roosevelt Hospital. Then Conner flagged down another cab and told the driver to take him to 145th and Amsterdam.

In the back of the taxi, Conner kept punching Angela's number into his phone's keypad. And no matter how many times he got the message saying, "This voice mail customer's message box is full; please try your call again later," he kept trying until the taxi stopped in front of the De La Rojas' apartment building.

"It's Conner," he shouted into the intercom. "I need to see Angie."

"She is not here, Conner," Gladys said.

"Buzz me in. It's important."

The door clicked open. Conner ran up the stairs to the apartment on the fourth floor. Angela's mother stood in front of the door wearing a housedress and shower clogs. Her hair was white, but in the hallway's fluorescents, its glow was lavender.

"Angie here?" Conner asked.

"No, Conner," said Gladys.

"Where is she?"

"I don't know."

"She's really not here?"

"No."

"Where did she go?"

"I don't know. She got a call."

"She got my calls? She listened to my messages?"

"I don't think so. She talked to someone and then she said she had to go."

"To where?"

"She didn't tell me."

"Did she say when she's coming back?"

"As soon as she can."

"Where's Atticus?" asked Conner.

"The child is sleeping."

"Can I see him?"

Gladys stepped back from the doorway. Conner walked past her, into the room where a crib was stationed beside a bed that had once been Angie's. On the few nights Conner had stayed over, even after they had gotten engaged, he had not been allowed to sleep in this room. He had slept on the living-room couch, which was a few inches shorter than he was. Now, as he stared at his son's face, Conner could see his wife's cheekbones, her luminescent black hair. Friends and family often said that Atticus had his father's eyes, but those eyes were closed, and as for that peaceful expression on the boy's face as he slept, Conner couldn't say whether that belonged to him or to Angela. If either of them had ever looked so calm, both he and Angela had lost that feeling long ago. He wished he could rest in the bed beside the cot until the boy woke up. But in his pocket, he had a key to an apartment, which contained the manuscripts that, along with the flash drive, could help to convince Angie and the police that his story was true. And in his coat, he had a gun with one bullet gone.

"I'll be back for you, buddy," Conner whispered to his son. "As soon as I can. I'm gonna leave you for just a little while, but after I'm back, I'll try my best to never leave you again."

He kissed Atticus's forehead, ran his hand through the boy's hair. And then he walked out of the bedroom. Conner borrowed a shoe-box and a suitcase from his mother-in-law. In the bathroom, he unloaded the gun, and placed it and the bullets in the suitcase along with his coat. He knew he could carry a gun in his checked luggage as long as it wasn't loaded—Cole Padgett did it all the time.

49

The flight from LaGuardia was fast and smooth, and the skies were so clear that, as Conner looked out his window, it seemed as though the plane were flying upside down and the lights he was seeing were coming not from towns and cities but from planets and stars. He passed over Pennsylvania and Ohio. On some level, he was aware of all the drama in the lives that must have been going on below him. Yet at the same time, he found himself unable to conceive of those lives from this distant vantage point, even when he passed over a tiny slice of Indiana, the state in which the events of my last half decade had been playing out—a small version of Conner's story, a tale of lives upended by words.

When he got to O'Hare, he picked up his luggage at the baggage claim. He unzipped the suitcase in a men's-room stall. He took out his coat, put it on, loaded the gun, and placed it in a pocket. He

wheeled the empty suitcase to the taxi stand; no one else was waiting in line.

"Where to, my good friend?" the taxi driver asked as Conner
got in.

"Six-Eighty Lake Shore."

The driver laughed. "Used to be *seeks-seeks-seeks*," he said.

"I've heard that," said Conner.

The driver had an Eastern European accent, and for a moment,
Conner feared that everything that had just happened in New York
had been a fantasy, and now Pavel Bilski was driving him to be
ambushed by Dex. But upon closer inspection in the rearview, the
taxi driver—Sy Radosevich was printed on his license—had very
little in common with Dudek, save for the accent and eyebrows.
Conner wondered who this man had been before he started driving
a cab. Maybe he had been a writer too, one who had also disappeared. Maybe cities were filled with writers leading double lives, all
of them secretly working for Dex.

A black limousine was parked in front of 680 Lake Shore Drive,
but Conner paid it little mind. The doorman greeted Conner by
name, but Conner was walking past him too quickly to register
whether or not the name on his brass plate really was Pynchon.

Conner took the gun out of his coat pocket as he rode the elevator up, held it firmly in his right hand. He stepped out onto the
penthouse floor and wheeled his empty suitcase forward. It whirred
softly over the carpet. Conner took Dex's key out of his pocket as
he approached the apartment, and was surprised his hands weren't
shaking. He brought the key toward the lock, but as he inserted it,
the door gave way.

Conner froze for a moment. Then, he pushed the door open
the rest of the way, leaving his suitcase just outside in the hallway.
The door opened without even a creak. The apartment was dark

as Conner stepped gingerly across the soft carpet. He felt his way through the hallway, past the Norman Mailer bullet hole, then into the library. Even though he could barely make out any of the furniture, he knew where he was going. He had mapped the apartment inside his mind. He would navigate his way past the chairs in the library, and when he reached the bookcase, he would use the butt of the gun to smash the glass. He would grab the manuscripts, run for the hallway, drop them in his suitcase, zip it, run for the stairs, then through the lobby, out the front door. He would catch a cab to O'Hare, drop the gun in the trash when he got to the airport, take the next plane to LaGuardia, then head back to Gladys's apartment; surely Angie would be back by then.

He felt his way along the wall and stopped when he reached the bookcase. He could picture the small, locked glass doors in front of the manuscripts. He put out his hand just to make sure that he was in the right place. But there was no glass where there should have been; instead, he felt varnished wood. Where bound manuscripts should have been was empty space. He moved his hand gently through air, then felt something sharp slice the back of his hand. Broken glass. Conner winced, felt blood ooze from his skin. He touched the bottom of a shelf—there were jagged shards. The bookcase had been smashed open. Conner stepped back, felt his way along the wall. He was looking for a light switch when a voice split open the silence.

"Put it down," the voice said.

Not Dex's voice. Though the voice was low, it clearly belonged to a woman. "The gun," the woman said. "Put it the fuck down." Conner gripped the gun more tightly, but then a shot shattered one of the windows that gave out onto Lake Michigan. Conner lowered his hand, and when the voice ordered him once more to put down the gun, he placed it on the table.

The room turned bright. One of the desk lamps had been switched on; it illuminated the library in an eerie green glow. Now Conner could see that there were no manuscripts in the bookcase; it was empty—the glass plate had been shattered and slivers were lying not only on the shelves of the bookcase but also on the carpet beneath it. At the head of the table, Dex was lying facedown, a pool of black blood flowing out from under him. In the blood, Conner could see reflections of the illuminated desk lamp, bursts of green and white light like stars in a blood-black sky. Conner made as if to run toward Dex, but the voice stopped him: "Don't."

Conner turned slowly. He could now see the face of the woman who was holding the gun on him; she, too, seemed to glow faintly green.

"Margot Hetley," he said.

50

There sat the author of the Wizard Vampire Chronicles series—regal, enraged, like a betrayed queen. She wore a green-black dress that set off her green-blond hair; around her neck was a strand of greenish pearls. On the table in front of her was a green-black bag filled with greenly glowing manuscripts. In one hand, she held a green-black gun.

I know certain individuals who would be very interested in the books you have written, Dex had said. Conner had not been thinking of Margot Hetley, but maybe he should have—he thought of the random violence that blazed through her novels, all the soulless intercourse, all the gratuitous gore; he thought of her fierce gaze when their eyes had met at Shascha Books—*tell the cunt to get in line.* The only other person who had broken her contract, Dex had said. He had repaid her with the crime Conner had written, but

Pavel was gone and so was Dex's protection. Conner could hear Dex's low, strangled breaths.

"Stand right there—*still*—and empty your pockets, mate," Margot said, and when Conner did not comply, she gripped the gun hard with both hands. "I said empty your fucking pockets."

Conner took out his wallet, his change, and after Margot told him to "take out the bleedin' rest," he pulled out the flash drive and slid it across the table toward Margot. She snatched it and smiled a knowing, crooked smile. "You. Thievin'. Little. Wank," she said.

"I'm not," said Conner. "All I did was write."

"Oh, I read what you wrote, mate." Margot reached into her shoulder bag and pulled out *The Embargoed Manuscript*. "Your friend Dex, he told me all about it."

"Not my friend," said Conner.

"Yeah, not anyone's friend anymore." Margot jutted her chin in the direction of the body slumped upon the table. Dex's breaths were coming more slowly, as if he were hooked up to a failing ventilator. "Now," she said, "back up against the window, real slow."

Conner took a step back. He felt his legs quiver. He could make a run toward her, try to wrest the gun away, he thought. But he didn't like his chances. He took another small step backward.

"Margot," he said.

No response.

"Ms. Hetley."

Nothing.

"Look," he said.

"What?"

"It was just supposed to be a story, that's all."

Margot held up the flash drive. "What's this then? *Your* story?"

Conner tried to explain what had actually happened, but he couldn't convince Margot of its truth any more than he had been able to convince Angela. He had lost his ability to tell a story people could believe. If he had been smart enough to write a perfect crime, how could he have been dumb enough to not know Dex would try to commit it?

"But you know how it works," Conner said. "He never told me."

"What?" asked Margot. "That he'd actually do it?"

"That's right."

"Are you taking the piss?" She pointed a long, erect index finger at him. "Are you that bloody stupid? Or are you just that bad of a liar?"

Conner felt his breaths coming faster; his chest felt tight. "I could pay you back," he said.

"With what?" asked Margot.

"The money he paid me. The $2.5 million. I've still got most of it."

"What about the other half?" asked Margot.

"What other half?"

"You think that's all he got? A measly $2.5 mil?"

"Please," Conner said. "I have a wife and a son."

"World's full of wives and children. Nothing but," said Margot. "'Fraid that'll be their loss."

"But I have the same editor as you do."

"You mean you used to." Margot cocked the gun. "No, mate," she said, "you hurt me real bad, and now I'm gonna hurt you worse."

His back was up against the glass. One bullet and he'd smash through the window, down thirty stories, accelerating until he reached the pavement. He wondered if he would die before he hit the ground or if he would feel conscious of every moment of his descent. He ran for Margot as she pulled the trigger, but the moment she did, someone blasted through the doorway and leaped toward her.

"What the fuck?" Margot Hetley pivoted toward the intruder, but it was too late; Angela De La Roja was on her in a flash.

51

It happened too fast for Conner to be sure he wasn't dreaming it, that this wasn't some lovely scene he was imagining as he was actually falling down to Lake Shore Drive. It happened too fast for Conner to ask Angie how she had gotten there, if she had listened to his messages and finally believed his story. Before Conner had even made it from one side of the room to the other, Angie had wrestled Margot to the floor, disarmed her, cracked her across the face with the butt of a gun, then lifted up the internationally renowned, widely translated, award-winning, bestselling novelist of Wizard Vampire Chronicles volumes one through nine and threw her back into her chair. She trained one gun on Margot and passed the other to Conner. She checked Dex's throat for a pulse. "Call 911," she said.

Conner pulled out his phone. He began to key in the number. Margot laughed.

"Call the fucking bobbies?" Margot asked. "And tell them what?" Her lip was bleeding—that crooked smile she usually flashed for paparazzi looked even more sinister.

"What do you think, mate?" Margot asked as Conner pressed a 9 and a 1 on his phone. "You think they'll come after me? When there's $2.5 mil in *your* bank account, your fingerprints on a gun and my flash drive, and a manuscript telling all what you done?"

Conner didn't key in the last 1 on the phone. He looked at Margot; Angie did too. Even with her lip bleeding, a man dying across from her, and two guns aimed at her, Margot knew how to tell a story that would make you listen.

"No, that's not the story," she said. "The way I see it is that you and this toffer Dex was in on it all along; you came here to get your manuscript, then ice him. Anyway, that's the way I'll tell it, and believe me, mate, I know a fair bit about storytelling, a fair bit more than you. I read your work, mate. Much as I could get through. Bloody amateur. Nice details, dull plot. Shascha asked me to blurb it. I told her no bloody chance. I know what stories people will believe. Margot Hetley shot a man who stole her flash drive? That ain't one of 'em."

Angie was backing her way toward Dex, keeping the gun pointed at Margot, but Conner was wavering. How much money could Margot throw at lawyers? He would probably wind up getting jail time, and Margot would sell a million more books. Maybe she could even get a memoir deal. He wondered what that memoir might be called. Then an idea hit him.

"Write it down," he told Margot.

"What?" asked Angie.

Conner opened a drawer and produced a sheet of Dex's stationery and a fountain pen. He thrust them in front of Margot.

"Write down everything that happened," said Conner. "The real story."

233

"What the hell for? You're coercing me, mate; you're pointing guns."

"I don't give a shit. Write it down." Conner pointed the gun at her heart.

"Conner," Angie began, but he wouldn't let her finish the sentence. It was the only way he could think of, he said. Margot was a good storyteller; people would believe the story she told.

"Do it. Write it down. And tell the truth—all of it," he said. "Details. Give every detail."

"Or you'll what? Shoot me?"

"You're fucking right I will."

Margot believed him. He still had that talent—reflected what other people thought of themselves, and surely, in his place, Margot would not have hesitated. She began to write while Angie made her way to the head of the table, where Dex was still lying facedown. Angie pulled him up, ripped open his shirt. There was a bullet hole in his neck as big as the one in his wall, and blood was seeping out. She tried to use one of his shirtsleeves to staunch the bleeding.

"Breathe," she told Dex. *"Breathe."*

Dex looked every bit of his seventy-five years now, maybe even ten years older. His mouth was open, frozen in a mask of disbelief, as if he couldn't believe a story about him could actually come true. His eyes were bloodshot, filmy; his chest looked hollow and the skin stretched over his ribs looked thin and used up.

Angie called 911 as Conner kept his attention fixed on Margot and what she was writing; he kept pressing her to add more details, the sorts of details that would make people believe her story. He told Margot he wanted addresses; he wanted her flight number; he wanted to know where she had sat on the plane; he wanted to know who had sat next to her, where she had hired her limo, who the driver was.

"And don't make any of it up, 'cause you know I'll fact-check the fuck out of everything," he said.

"All this'll never help you, mate," said Margot. Conner moved behind her, looked over her shoulder, followed the swooping, swirling path of her pen. He studied the words she was writing more closely. His eyes widened; he swallowed hard.

"Holy mother of Christ," he said.

Angie had ripped the other sleeve of Dex's shirt; the first sleeve was drenched in blood; now blood was seeping onto this one too. "What?" she asked.

"She can't spell." Conner stared at the words on the page. Even in this moment, the revelation was dumbfounding. All the books Margot had written—were they really hers, or someone else's creation? "The bestselling author in the English language," Conner said softly, "and she can't even spell."

"The story's what matters; spelling's overrated, you cunt," Margot said. She thrust her pen into Conner's guts, grabbed his gun hand, slammed it down on the table. Conner yelled. The gun came loose. Margot grabbed it, snatched her bag of manuscripts, raced for the door, fired the gun, then dashed down the hall, bound for the stairwell.

"Christ! Ange! *Goddammit!* Shit!" Conner looked down at his palm. A hole had been blown right through it, and dark blood was flowing out. Angie reached for his hand, led him fast into the hallway. He was trailing blood on the carpet; his shirt was stained with blood and ink. Through his white shirt was a black ink hole where Margot had stabbed him with her pen. The black and the red were intermingling. There was no sign of Margot in the hallway save for one of the manuscripts, which had fallen out of her bag. When Conner and Angie got down to Lake Shore Drive, ambulances and police cars were already there—lights flashing,

sirens blaring. A doorman named Pynchon was directing paramedics up to the penthouse.

"When did you realize I was telling you the truth?" Conner asked
Angie breathlessly. "When you listened to my messages?"

"No," said Angie. "When Margot Hetley called me looking for
you." She reached out to hail a cab.

52

This all happened last night?" I asked Conner.

It was past midnight. I wanted to get back home to my kids. My mother seemed overwhelmed by everything these days, even more so late at night, and I had a hard time imagining her getting Ramona or Beatrice to sleep. The Coq d'Or was still going strong; there must have been a convention in town. I was trying to imagine my father having once been in the crowd, but couldn't figure out which of the men he might have been or become. It didn't occur to me then that that person might have been me.

"Yeah," Conner said. "It happened last night."

He and Angie had rushed to Northwestern Memorial Hospital, where he was treated for the gunshot wound, but they had ducked out after the doc had said he would have to report the incident. The wound didn't seem grave; he would just have to wear a bandage for a few more weeks. Angie had already gone back to New York, and Conner would fly back tomorrow. He could have flown with Angie, but he had wanted to stay a little while longer.

"What for?" I asked.

"So you and I could talk."

"I didn't realize I was that important to you."

Conner drained his beer. "You're the only one who can tell the story," he said.

"No, I'm not," I said. "*You* could tell it."

"Nah, I'm done," he said. "We're heading out. I'm not gonna be a target my whole life." He, Angie, and Atticus were going to disappear for a while. He was done with literary agents, lawyers, and publishers. The moment he started writing his story or trying to get people to publish it, he ran the risk of blowing his cover. Margot Hetley would find him. Maybe Dex would too.

"Isn't Dex dead?" I asked.

"Maybe, maybe not," said Conner. "The paramedics were just showing up when Angie and I got outta there. He was still breathing."

"Where you going?" I asked. "Cornish, New Hampshire? Monroeville, Alabama? Mexico City?"

Conner looked as if I had caught him at something, but he forced a smile. "We don't know yet," he said. Wherever he was going, he hoped he wouldn't have to stay there forever, and the only chance he had to lead a normal life was for the whole story to get out. Someone had to write about everything that had happened with Dex and Jarosław Dudek and Margot Hetley, but since he couldn't write it himself, someone else had to do it.

"You're the only one who knows how to tell it," he said. "You're the only one who knows it and you're the only one I would trust with it."

For a moment, I found Conner's faith in stories quaint. When I first met him, he had said stories had saved his life.

"But what about me?" I asked.

"What about you?"

"I have a family too."

"Yeah, I know that, bud. That's why I'm here."

"But wouldn't I be in danger? Just like you are now?"

"How?"

"If someone finds out I'm writing the story."

Conner smiled. "You'll be fine. I've been trusting you all along, so you've got to trust me on that. By the time the story gets out into the world, it won't matter anymore anyway. I might even have a little surprise for you when you're done."

"What surprise?" I asked.

"You'll see," said Conner.

"And meanwhile, you're gonna be another recluse writer?" I asked. "Like your buddies Salinger, Pynchon, and Dudek?"

"Yeah, maybe. But with one big difference," said Conner.

"What's that?"

"People gave a damn about what happened to them."

"They might give a damn about you after they read the story," I said.

"You're getting the idea." Conner smiled as if I had already agreed to something, when the truth was that I hadn't decided. He shook my hand, then leaned across the table to embrace me, thumping me twice on the back.

"Well, I'm finally giving you your chance, pal," he said.

"What chance?" I asked. "To prove I can act like a decent human being?"

Conner nodded.

"I suppose you think that makes you a hero," I said.

"Depends how you write the story," said Conner.

IV:
Upon
Publication

I knew wherever I went, someone could find me. And I knew what-ever I wrote, someone might use it for reasons I never intended.

Adam Herstein Langer, *The Tenth Father*

53

I started writing the story about a week after my last meeting with Conner. I figured someone would buy it, and since neither Sabine nor I had found a job yet, we certainly needed however much money it might bring. Our house in Bloomington had been on the block for three months and we hadn't had an offer. The only people who showed up at our open house were our neighbors, the Macys and the Lahns, and some of my wife's soon-to-be-former colleagues, who came by to commiserate or gloat. Dr. Joel "Spag" Getty, who was now at Princeton but still had a couple of girlfriends in town, brought hash brownies and asked Sabine if anyone had ever told her she looked like Geena Davis in *Thelma & Louise*. Dr. Lloyd Agger popped by shirtless en route to a squash game and advised us to drop our asking price.

Meanwhile, Sabine and I were getting ready for our students' midterms while we waited to see which magazine or newspaper would hire me for an editorial gig, and which university might want to take Sabine on. But it was as shitty a time to be looking for work as it was to be selling a house. The unemployment rate had gone down a bit, sure, but only because people had abandoned their job searches. Yes, Sabine was a multilingual Ivy League product with nearly a decade's worth of experience at top-twenty schools, but none of the old geezers she should have been replacing were retiring—professors in their seventies had lost their savings in real estate or the stock market, and they had to keep working to support their spouses and their underemployed children. The best either of us had been able to come up with were adjunct teaching gigs in Chicago or northern New Jersey that paid five grand a semester. At home, all of us were getting on one another's nerves and I looked forward to the time I spent writing on my laptop at the Owlery, a vegetarian diner downtown where the owners were new to town and thankfully had no idea who I was.

Writing the story was easy, at least at first. I hadn't taken any notes during my conversations with Conner, but I had a good memory and so I just began writing it the way he had told it to me. The scene of Conner's confrontation with Margot Hetley was especially fun to write, though I did tone down some of her swearing. For the stories of the theft of the flash drive and also the bank heist in *Devil Shotgun* that had supposedly inspired Dex too, I gleaned some details from the newspaper accounts of those crimes, neither of which had ever been solved. As for the rest of the story, I relied solely on what Conner had told me. There was no mention of Dex Dunford in any of the biographies and articles I read about J. D. Salinger, Jarosław Dudek, Thomas Pynchon, Harper Lee, B. Traven, and the like, and neither could I find out anything about the stories they had written that had inspired Dex's crimes. Dex himself was impossible to locate. There were a few Dex Dunfords on Intelius.com, but none seemed to be the right one. And as for Conner, just about all the biographical information on the Internet had been lifted from the profile I had written about him for *Lit*. Other than his publisher's website, I was the only cited source on his *Wikipedia* entry and I had taken Conner's word for everything he had told me. On Lexis-Nexis and ProQuest, I did manage to find some of the articles he had written when he had worked as a crime reporter for the *New York Daily News*, so that stuff was true. And I found a notice regarding his marriage to Angela De La Roja in the *Morning Call*, but as for the rest of his biography—his childhood in South Philly, the time he spent in the US Navy, the college degree he'd gotten from Fordham—I couldn't find a thing. I found out even less about Angela.

Still, I didn't start trying to seriously research and verify Conner's story because I doubted it; I just wanted to make it more credible by adding the sorts of details Conner always worked into his own stories. In my own writing, I have always tended to be lazy; I wrote *Nine Fathers* as fiction because I had neither the desire nor the commitment to discover the true story; at *Lit*, I was master of the one-source profile: run the minidisc recorder; ship the disc to Bangalore for transcription; send it to the copyeditor; write a 150-word introduction and run that baby as a Q&A. But I thought I owed Conner something more. I truly wanted to believe the story because I liked Conner and I especially liked the faith he seemed to have in me. And to be completely honest, I also wanted the story to be true because I thought that would make it easier to sell.

But when I found myself unable to verify much of what Conner had told me, I became suspicious. Each problematic element of Conner's story was explainable in and of itself, but the sheer number of those elements was troubling. The fact that no Dex Dunford was living in the penthouse of 680 N. Lake Shore Drive was easy to explain; he might have died from his gunshot wounds, and even if he hadn't, he might not have wanted to return to that address. It didn't surprise me when I discovered that the doorman at 680 Lake Shore was a good deal younger than the man Conner had described, that his name wasn't Pynchon and that nothing was noteworthy about his teeth; Conner had told me "Pynchon" looked close to retirement and that he might have hallucinated the name anyway. I was unable to find any information in any crime blotters or on Everyblock.com about any gunshot victims at Northwestern Memorial Hospital on the night Margot Hetley had supposedly shot both Dex and Conner, but that information might not have been made public. Still, the cumulative effect of all these unexplained incidents made me wary, and more important, since I was writing nonfiction, I figured that they would rouse the suspicions of any even moderately scrupulous editor. I tried to get Conner on the phone, but the cell phone he called me from was no longer in service, and when I tried to find a number for a Conner Joyce in Delaware Water Gap, Pennsylvania, I learned his house was being sold and the real estate agent couldn't put me in touch with the seller, not even when I offered to pay her.

Ultimately, what made me doubt Conner's story more than anything else was the fact that he was relying on me to tell it. Who was I other than some random dude who had written one novel, edited a now-defunct magazine, and had been living as a house husband in Indiana? I had asked him "Why me?" and he had smiled and said, "I think you know why." And now I did. I was the schmuck who believed his stories, who took them at face value and never bothered to check if they were true, who one time fought my publisher to have the cigarettes airbrushed out of Conner's photos, who let him tell the story he wanted the world to believe.

The more I worked on writing Conner's story, the more I grew to resent him—the way he called me "buddy" and "pal," as if we had actually been friends; the way he talked about the millions Dex had paid him but never offered me any money, just told me that if I wrote the book, he might give me a "surprise." I resented the self-aggrandizing tone of his references to John Le Carré's novel *The Russia House*, as if he were a heroic master spy and I was a once-renowned but now disaffected publisher, when the truth was that we were just a couple of guys trying to make a buck—a common condition, to be sure, but hardly a noble one.

I picked up a copy of *The Russia House* from the Monroe County Public Library and I tried to read it, but I didn't get all the way through. I was too stressed out for a four-hundred-page Cold War espionage novel. I streamed the movie that starred Sean Connery and Michelle Pfeiffer instead, and as I did, one line resonated, but it wasn't the one about heroes and decent human beings. The line that kept echoing in my brain was spoken by an intelligence agent who realizes his spy is betraying him: "He's crossed over," the agent says. "My Joe's crossed over."

All this time, Conner had been setting me up, and though at first I wasn't sure what he had been setting me up for, the more I thought about it, the better idea I got. He had shown me the flash drive; it had been stolen, all right, but maybe he had done it himself; maybe everything he had told me about Dex was made up. Maybe Dex didn't even exist. Conner's publisher had let him go, Conner knew about the flash drive, and when the time was right he had committed the crime on his own. Maybe Angie had been in on it too; she was good with guns, and she knew enough from her time on the NYPD to understand that if they did it right, they could get away with it. "One crime," Cole Padgett had said. "A man can get away with any crime if he commits only one in his life. He just has to choose which one it will be." "I trust you," Conner had kept telling me. Wasn't that how all con artists operated—made you think they were putting all their trust in you so that you would trust them? I thought about when Beatrice had seen a picture of Conner in the aisle of the Borders and she had seemed frightened. I should have trusted the kid's instincts; they were always better than my own.

I kept writing the story, but it was no longer the story of a crime writer caught up in a plot that spun out of control when his book became the basis for a crime. Now the story was becoming one of a con artist who found his perfect mark in the form of a gullible Chicago-born, Indiana-based writer who would tell his tale and clear his name. I wasn't exactly sure who would buy that story, but I had a feeling somebody would. I could tell you I felt guilty about contemplating the idea of betraying someone I had considered a friend, but Conner had taken me for granted, had tried to take advantage of me, had treated me like a naïve sap.

As I neared the end of the story, I no longer considered the possibility that Conner might have been telling the truth—at least, not until I called up Shajilah Shascha Schapiro to tell her about the story I was writing, and she offered me $1.2 million for it.

"Double it," I said.

54

James Merrill Jr. Publishers was a once-esteemed boutique publisher that had fallen on hard times by the time it had published *Nine Fathers*. So I was looking forward to seeing the sleek interior of Schreiber & Sons. I wanted to ride the elevator up to Shascha's office. I wanted to watch all those important editors doing all their important work. I wanted to play the part of Pip in the old movie version of *Great Expectations*—I wanted to throw open Shascha's blinds and let in the light. But when I spoke with Courtney Guggenheim to set up a time to meet with Shascha, she said it wouldn't happen at her office. I wound up meeting them both on a bench near the carousel in Central Park, a few blocks away from S&S. That carousel had played an important role in *Catcher in the Rye*, but it didn't inspire any nostalgia in me, and not only because of my indifference to Salinger's work. Despite the lovely summer weather,

I found it a seedy spot, and being there without my kids made me feel like a creep. There was no calliope music; a tinny amplifier was playing Fine Young Cannibals tunes. I knew the publishing industry, like just about every other industry, was struggling, but still, I expected a little more fanfare for my second book than a meeting on a park bench where I had to buy my own Coke and talk loudly so I could be heard over "Ever Fallen in Love."

Shascha was already waiting on the park bench with Courtney when I arrived, checking her e-mail on her phone and flipping through manuscript pages. She was indeed striking—the sort of person who seemed used to having doors opened for her and voices going quiet the moment she entered a room. And Courtney Guggenheim was so lovely and polite that, like Conner, I couldn't help but wonder if she wasn't secretly plotting Shascha's overthrow. The two had dressed down for our meeting—Courtney wore jeans, sneakers, and a white VIRGINIA IS FOR LOVERS T-shirt; Shascha wore a belted black dress that looked as though she'd slept in it, and she kept her sunglasses on the whole time. Courtney shook my hand, but Shascha didn't even bother.

"You know where Conner is?" Shascha asked.

I said I didn't, then added, "Try Cornish, New Hampshire." Neither Courtney nor Shascha cracked a smile.

"How about Dex Dunford?" she asked.

"All I know is what I wrote," I said. "You've got it all down there."

Courtney nodded, but Shascha seemed resigned, as if she understood that I had told her everything I knew.

"Should we be talking to your agent?" asked Shascha. She spoke sharply yet quietly. I didn't feel like an author meeting his new editor; I felt like a narc wearing a wire.

"I don't have one," I said. "I used to."

"Who was it?"

I told her the agent's name and she snickered. "What about a lawyer?" she asked.

"Do I need one?"

"No. Better if you don't," she said. "We should keep this just between us." She gave Courtney a brief nod, and Courtney unzipped her purse and took out two copies of a contract that had been folded in three. I didn't look the documents over too carefully; to be honest, the only part that interested me was the money, and the number was the same one we had discussed. I never cared much about contracts; I figured people honored or broke them all the time, and whatever happened, I would do what I wanted and apologize for it later if I had to.

"Do I sign it now?" I asked.

Courtney handed me a pen. It wasn't a Salinger fountain pen; it was a crappy Bic. I signed both copies and handed them to Shascha, who signed and handed one back to me. Then Courtney handed me the check, which I folded and stuffed into my jeans.

I had other questions, but Shascha acted as if our business together was already finished.

"Might there be a movie deal in the future?" I asked. I thought Conner's story might make a pretty good film.

"You're giving us all those rights; we'll handle that," said Shascha.

"And what about selling the story overseas?" I asked. Millions of people were fascinated by Margot's stories; I felt sure they would want to know the story behind the crime.

"We'll deal with all that, too," Shascha said.

Shascha didn't have anything to say when I asked about book covers or publicity campaigns or any revisions she might want me to make. The contract looked much shorter than any I had ever seen. There were no installments, just one lump sum paid "upon signing," plus the confidentiality agreement that forbade me from discussing the contents of the book with anyone before it was published.

"Are you going to want me to do any speaking engagements? Interviews? Book tours?" I liked imagining Sabine, Ramona, Beatrice, and I flipping channels and ordering room service in hotel suites.

"It's too early to talk about that," said Shascha.

"Why?" I tried to look directly at her, but all I saw in her sunglasses was my own reflection. It was then that I realized Shascha wasn't buying my book at all; she was buying my silence, and the reason was because she knew Conner's story was true. Margot Hetley was the franchise, and she had to protect the franchise at any cost. As long as no one learned Margot's story, the franchise was safe. Shascha had the rights to the story; she could publish it or not, change it or leave it as it was. I had signed away my rights in exchange for the check, and I had nothing more to say in the matter. I felt a little twinge of guilt, and a little sorry I hadn't asked for even more money. But I sensed I'd get over all that. I tried to peek at the manuscript pages Shascha was holding. I thought I saw the name "Dudek" on the title page, but my eyes were probably deceiving me.

"Are you ever going to publish my book at all?" I asked Shascha. "Are you ever going to let anyone know the real story?"

Shascha got up from the bench and started walking away, but Courtney Guggenheim told me all I needed to know. I could hear her singing over the music that was blaring from the carousel—*"Dee-dah-dee-dah-dee."*

55

Well, you screwed me, pal," Conner told me with a heavy sigh. "You screwed me big-time."

I had wondered when or if word would get back to Conner that I had written his story but had sold it to Shascha. I wondered what he would think if and when he learned no one would ever read it aside from Shascha, Courtney, and me.

For the first few days after I returned to Indiana from my trip to New York, I felt nervous and had the distinct sensation that cars were following me, but I may have just imagined it. After Shascha's check cleared, I turned my attention to more pressing matters, such as walking the dog, dealing with Ramona's and Beatrice's ear infections, getting one or both kids out of the house so that Sabine could write some more job applications, and trying to figure out what we would do with our lives. At least now, with the money Shascha had paid me, we had time to try to figure that out.

I was in Chicago. My kids and I were visiting my mother for Fourth of July weekend while Sabine was in Bloomington to oversee yet another open house. Ramona was with my mom at the North Park Village Nature Center and I was pushing Beatrice's stroller through Lincoln Park Zoo when I became conscious of a presence behind me. The presence became considerably more noticeable as I approached the coyote habitat. Beatrice had fallen asleep shortly after we got out of the car, so I hadn't really been looking at animals, just pushing the stroller so that she would stay asleep.

The coyote was small—a good deal smaller than my own dog. His fur looked coarse and reddish-brown, and I was staring into his indifferent ice-blue eyes when Conner approached me; his hair was nearly all white now. He was wearing a pressed white shirt with the sleeves rolled up and new blue jeans. He carried a black backpack over one shoulder.

"If I were a different sort of guy, I'd do something right now, buddy," he said.

"Like what?" I asked.

"I dunno. Like kick your ass or something. Isn't that what I'm supposed to do?"

I had never seen him angry before. I tried to match my rage to his.

"If I were a different sort of guy, I wouldn't have believed your story in the first place, *buddy*, and I would've kicked your ass for that," I said. I had learned from dealing with my wife's former colleagues in Indiana—if you met hostility with hostility and stood your ground, people usually backed down whether you were right or not.

Conner squinted at me. He raised his right hand as if he were about to make a fist, then dropped his arm to his side.

"What're you talking about, man?" he asked. "I don't even get you."

"What do you think?" I asked.

"If I knew, I'd tell you," he said.

We stood there in front of the coyote, who gazed out at us from atop his stone perch, and I told Conner what I meant. I told him I really had started out trying to write the story the way he had told it, but I had stopped believing it, had become convinced he had lied to me. I said that I had read *The Russia House* and I kept thinking about that one line—"He's crossed over. My Joe's crossed over."

"That's in the goddamn movie," he said. "That's not even in the book."

Nevertheless, I pressed on, and as I did, the color began to fade from Conner's cheeks and his eyes looked softer. I had always said people looked at me and saw what they thought of themselves, and the same was true of Conner. I had looked into Conner's eyes and seen a liar; he was looking into my eyes and seeing a guy who told the truth. Maybe neither of us had the slightest sense of who the other man was; maybe all we could see were versions of ourselves.

"So, when did you start to think maybe I wasn't lying," Conner asked.

"When Shascha offered to pay me two million bucks to keep me from publishing it," I said. "What would you have done in my position? Told the story or taken the dough? If Angela hadn't found out about the flash drive, you wouldn't have said a word to her about it. Besides, I might've gone along with it if I hadn't realized how little you thought of me." There was nothing for me to lose anymore, so I told him everything I had kept to myself during the times we had spent together: I knew why he had chosen me—because I was gullible and had weak morals. I knew it didn't have anything to do with my skill as a writer or even with the fact that he thought of me as a friend; he just knew I was one lazy sucker.

Conner cocked his head to one side and studied my face as if he had seen something on it he hadn't expected to find there.

"You mean you don't know?" he finally asked. "You're not pretending. It's not that you just don't like talking about it; you really don't know."

"Know what?" I asked.

"Why I asked you."

"But I do," I said. "I just told you."

Conner smiled and shook his head as if he just now realized that he had spent his life as the butt of a cruel practical joke, but it had been going on so long that all he could do was laugh.

"You think that's what it's about? Really?" he asked.

"What else could there be?"

Conner took off his backpack and laid it on the sidewalk. He crouched down, unzipped the backpack, and as he did, he asked, "Do you remember what I told you about the surprise I might give you after you wrote the book?"

"Sure," I said, "and I didn't like your condescending little enticement. In fact, that pissed me off too."

"I didn't think I'd give this to you," he said. "I didn't think you deserved it. But now I don't think I have a choice."

"What is it?" I asked.

"I don't know anymore," he said. "Maybe it's your legacy."

He reached into the backpack and pulled out a bound, typewritten manuscript. It was about two hundred and some-odd pages long; the paper looked thin, yellowed, and brittle, and there were a pair of small, reddish-brown splotches upon it that could have been ink and could have been blood.

"What the hell is this?" I took the manuscript and stared at it.

Its title was *The Missing Glass*, but that's not what made me stop dead and look at the page with such confusion and fear that even the coyote must have sensed my turmoil because he started to howl. I felt pale, dizzy.

"No," I finally said. "It can't be real."

"It is," he said.

"I thought you said Salinger wrote this," I said.

Conner winked at me. "He did," he said. "Don't you see? He did."

"But . . ." I didn't complete the sentence. There was one name on the spine, but the other one on the title page caught my eye—Sid J. Langer. My mom had always had a thing about anagrams, but I was never much good at them. I kept messing around the letters in my head, spelling them one way and then the other—Sid J. Langer. J. D. Salinger. In some absurd way, it made sense. Like all solutions to mysteries, it explained both everything and nothing at the same time.

"Revelatory," Conner had written when he had blurbed *Nine Fathers*. "Keeps all its secrets until the very end, which is a whopper." I had no idea what he might have meant until this very moment. A reader can understand so much more about a story than the author himself.

I tried to think of anything to say that would keep me from fainting. "Did you read it?" I asked.

"On the plane, yeah," said Conner.

"Where were you coming from?" I asked.

"I'm not telling you that, pal," said Conner. "I don't trust you that much."

"How is it?" I asked. "The book."

"Not his best. Crime wasn't his thing. But there's a part of the story that'll probably interest you."

"What part?"

"About a writer, pretty well known. He comes to Chicago, meets a cocktail waitress at a nice hotel. They have a kid together. He agrees to support the boy and give her money whenever she asks, but on one condition—she never tells her son or anyone else who the real father is. You could say there was kind of an unwritten contract between them."

"That's a fucked-up story," I said.

"True ones usually are," said Conner. "Man, I figured you had to know. You wrote that whole book; it's so obvious."

"Not to me, apparently," I said.

"Anyway, that's the reason I wanted you," Conner said. "His son. I wanted his son to write my story. Dex knew it too—but he'd already signed an agreement saying he'd never mess with one of his sons."

"His sons?"

"Yeah, sons. That's what he made Dex put in the contract."

I took a breath, tried to slow my heart. "Well," I said, "I guess his son did wind up telling your story."

"Yeah, I suppose you did do that," Conner said. "Didn't turn out quite the way I was planning."

"Right. But then again, *Catcher in the Rye* didn't either," I said.

"How's that?"

"Book winds up in the back pockets of killers," I said. "I doubt old Sid J. Langer was planning for that."

"Well, sometimes you don't have control," Conner said. "Actually, you never do. You write a book and people use it in ways and for things you never dreamed." He slapped the manuscript with his palm. "You should read it."

"I don't know," I said. "I'm kind of afraid to." I knew the manuscript was worth millions, but I didn't want to look at it now. I knew it could tell me some of the secrets I had spent my life trying to discover, but I didn't want to hear them anymore. I put the manuscript in the basket of my daughter's stroller. She was still sleeping and the coyote was still howling.

"Man, I'm sorry, dude," I told Conner.

258

"For what?"

"I fucked you over. You're right."

"You didn't know."

"Doesn't matter. I should've trusted. I'll try to make it right."

"Little too late for that, buddy," said Conner.

"I'm not sure," I said.

"You don't have it in you to be a hero," he said.

"Yeah," I said. "Maybe a decent human being, though."

I shook his hand, and he pulled me close. I felt his whiskers against my cheek as he thumped me on the back.

"So how does it feel?" I asked. "Being a recluse writer; is it just like you dreamed?"

"Wish I knew," he said. "I'm not a recluse; I'm more like a fugitive. Maybe I can be a recluse one day."

Then he told me he had a plane to catch, and I knew not to ask him where he was going. All I needed to know was that he and Angie were still together and Atticus was well. I wished him luck.

Conner told me that we might not meet again, but I didn't believe that. Somehow, I figured our paths would cross and probably even sooner than either of us would like. Margot was undoubtedly looking for him, Shascha too, maybe even Dex, but I thought I could find a way to protect Conner, honor the unwritten contract I had with him. I watched Conner walk through the zoo, hands in the pockets of his jeans. When he had exited the gates and turned out of sight, I could hear my daughter stirring in her stroller.

"Dad?" she asked. She looked frightened.

"Yes, Bea?"

"I heard talking."

"No," I said. "It was just a coyote."

POSTSCRIPT

Conner had given me the idea. It was the same basic one he had given Dex when he'd written *The Embargoed Manuscript*. But I wanted to use that idea to save somebody, not to rob them. The thief in Conner's novel—and Dex and Pavel in real life—had stolen a flash drive. They set up a website, leaked word that they could provide pirated editions of the new Wizard Vampire Chronicles book. They took credit-card orders, transferred the money to their bank account, clicked Send All, then shut down the site. Selling over the Internet was easy; the hard part was convincing people you had something they wanted to buy.

I didn't care only about the money. I might even have given away the true story about Conner Joyce but for the fact that I didn't think people would have given it too much attention unless I charged something. I wanted people to believe, *really believe*. So I spent a lot of time proofreading the manuscript, typesetting it, formatting it so that people could read it on an iPad, a Kindle, or a Nook. When I was done, I put the word out on Twitter, Facebook, and Google+. If people wanted to hear the true story about the theft of WVCIX, I said, all it would take was ten bucks and a credit card.

At first, everyone assumed my story was a hoax, and during the first few days, I sold only a couple dozen copies. But then, after people started reading it, they began posting reviews, and although most of them were positive, the negative ones were just as powerful because people were really starting to discuss it; even if they didn't like the story or the way I wrote it or the way I had characterized Margot Hetley, most seemed to take it for granted that it was true. I guess the details and the little personal touches were what convinced them—my descriptions of Shascha and of Courtney Guggenheim, of the doorman at 680 N. Lake Shore Drive, of my wife's colleagues, and our Buck Floomington blog, and that last scene in the zoo with my daughter waking up after Conner left and me telling her that she hadn't heard voices, only a coyote.

I tried talking to my mother about everything that happened, but she didn't want to discuss it. Her memory really was fading, or she was doing a very good job of pretending it was. To me, she had always been a puzzle and always would be. That I had found out who my dad really was didn't change the fact that she had made a promise to him that she wasn't going to break, not even after he had cut her off financially, and not even after he had died. She wouldn't read *The Missing Glass*. "I already know that story; why would I want to read about it?" she asked.

I asked her what I should do with the manuscript, and she gave the same answer Dex would have given: "Burn it."

I should probably tell you I felt guilty about violating my agreement with Shascha. After all, I had taken her money. I should probably tell you I had some reservations about accusing Margot Hetley of a crime without any actual proof. But I felt a greater responsibility to Conner; one time, long ago when he was just a boy, he wrote a letter to my father and never got a response, which was in some way how I had spent my life—asking questions and waiting for answers that I finally gave up hoping would ever come.

I knew that one day it might all catch up with me, but I didn't hide. I didn't pack up my family and move out of the country. I didn't change my name; I even kept my phone number listed. I took our house off the market, figuring we would hunker down and wait to sell until the end of the global depression or whatever it was that we seemed to be going through. I knew wherever I went, someone could find me. And I knew whatever I wrote, someone might use it for reasons I never intended. Maybe they would use it to find Conner, or maybe they would use it to find me, or maybe my story would give them an idea for a crime. I didn't really give a damn. If someone wanted to track me down and confront me, I would deal with all that when the time came.

It happened at my father's gravesite. I had gone there not so much to pay my respects as to try to make manifest a story that still seemed to exist only in my own mind. But as far as that was concerned, visiting the New Hampshire cemetery didn't do much good—the name engraved on the headstone was just one more name in a cemetery full of them. Whether the name was J. D. Salinger or Sid J. Langer or something totally different didn't matter. Some of the gravesites had flowers on them, but his didn't and I hadn't brought any, just a manuscript completed right around the time I was born.

I was laying the manuscript atop the earth before the gravestone when I saw Dex approaching. He wore a pinstriped navy-blue suit with a pale-yellow pocket square. He looked scrawnier and older than Conner had described. But I recognized him by the long, wide scar on his neck and the yellow-eyed falcon atop his walking stick. Conner had made that walking stick seem like an affectation, but now Dex seemed to need it. Pavel Bilski was gone, taking Jarosław Dudek along with him; maybe that's why Dex looked so alone.

"Mr. Dunford," I said, and he smiled, perhaps surprised I already knew who he was. We talked by the grave, and he told me of all the trouble Conner and I had caused him. I was not surprised when he told me I would have to devise some way to compensate him. And I had already prepared my response.

"Why don't I write you a book?" I said.

"A book?"

I nodded.

"What sort?" he asked.

"A perfect crime," I said.

"Just one copy?" he asked.

"Manual typewriter," I said. "No copies, no carbons."

"Yes," said Dex, "that's it exactly."

He held my glance for quite some time.

"What would you like me to write about?" I asked.

"I'm not the writer," said Dex.

"I know," I said. "But why don't you try anyway?"

"All right," he said. And after he had considered for a while, he said, "Why don't you start with this? Somewhere in this world, there is a very rich, very ruthless, very powerful woman who stole some priceless manuscripts from me and nearly killed me in the process. Those manuscripts are very dear to me, and I would very much like to get the damned things back."

He then gestured to the manuscript on my father's grave. "You can start by giving that one back to me, Adam. It's mine, you know."

And so I handed it to him.

Conner Joyce had told me he felt some compunction about writing that first novel for Dex. He said he wouldn't have done it save for the fact that he had no other choice. I did have choices, but I wanted to do it anyway. I already had an idea for a story that would get Dex what he wanted. And I knew that, at least for me, inspiring one person was just as good as inspiring thousands. I didn't really care who that person was or what I would or wouldn't inspire him to do. I really didn't mind that I would be working for Dex now; a man does what he has to do in order to protect and provide for his family. And as one of Conner's favorite writers told him, in one way or the other, we all wind up working for Dex.

ACKNOWLEDGMENTS

Thanks to everyone who helped me in one way or another to create this book, especially the Langer, Sissenich, and Langer-Sissenich families. My heartfelt thanks also go out to Maria Braeckel, Campus View Child Care Center, Thomas Conner, Beth Dembitzer, Laura De Silva, Gina Fattore, Jane Friedman, Terry Govan and Mark Leuschner, Richard Green, Amy Hackenberg and Erik Tillema, Harmony School, Julianne Hausler, the *Jewish Daily Forward*, Cynthia Joyce, Gretchen Koss, Jerome Kramer, Hana Landes, the Lahn family, the Macy Family, Nicholas Meyer, Nicole Passage, Tina Pohlman, Michael Radulescu, Marly Rusoff, Martha Sharpe, Anjali Singh, Corinne Smith, Cindy Spiegel, Amy Watts, and Michelle Weiner. And, of course, many, many thanks for the inspiration provided by the Chicago Public Library, the Coq d'Or Lounge of the Drake Hotel, Feast Bakery Café, the Hungarian Pastry Shop, the Monroe County Public Library, and the Uptown Café of Bloomington, Indiana.

ABOUT THE AUTHOR

Born and raised in Chicago, Adam Langer is the author of the novels *Crossing California*, *The Washington Story*, *Ellington Boulevard*, and *The Thieves of Manhattan*, and the memoir *My Father's Bonus March*. He has written about books and authors for such publications as the *Chicago Tribune*, the *Los Angeles Times*, the *New York Times*, the *Huffington Post*, the *San Francisco Chronicle*, and the *Washington Post*, among others. He has been a frequent radio and TV guest, including appearances on CNN, Fox, and NPR's *Morning Edition* and *All Things Considered*. The Chicago Public Library recently purchased a significant collection of his papers. He is the former senior editor of *Book Magazine* and currently serves as the arts and culture editor of the *Jewish Daily Forward*. Langer lives in New York City with his wife, Beate; his daughters, Nora and Solveig; and their dog, Kazoo.

OPEN ROAD
INTEGRATED MEDIA

Open Road Integrated Media is a digital publisher and multimedia content company. Open Road creates connections between authors and their audiences by marketing its ebooks through a new proprietary online platform, which uses premium video content and social media.

Videos, Archival Documents, and New Releases

Sign up for the Open Road Media newsletter and get news delivered straight to your inbox.

Sign up now at
www.openroadmedia.com/newsletters

FIND OUT MORE AT
WWW.OPENROADMEDIA.COM

FOLLOW US:
@openroadmedia and
Facebook.com/OpenRoadMedia

CPSIA information can be obtained at www.ICGtesting.com
Printed in the USA
BVOW08s0600070813

327620BV00003BB/5/P